Time Rock
Red Warp II

Don DeBon

Time Rock
Red Warp II
Don DeBon

First Printing
Copyright © 2015 Don DeBon

ISBN 978-0-9881783-7-3
ISBN 978-0-9881783-5-9 (e-book)

Dedicated to the one special woman in my life who convinced me to take up my pen again.

Not to mention my wonderful editors. This book would not have been possible without you.

Contents

Chapter 1   1

Chapter 2   10

Chapter 3   15

Chapter 4   23

Chapter 5   28

Chapter 6   57

Chapter 7   92

Chapter 8   113

Chapter 9   140

Chapter 10   177

Chapter 11   204

Chapter 12   209

Professor Keleeigan sat over one of his consoles tweaking several wave guides on the display. He rolled his chair over to a large piece of equipment filled to the brim with various circuits and electronics. He carefully reached inside and soldered a new chip into place. The status lights on the box continued to flash orange for a few more minutes, then blinked green. "There," he grunted, "it is finally finished." A knock at the door brought him out of his thoughts as he walked through the maze of tables and equipment that covered the lighthouse floor. Pulling open the heavy wooden door he smiled as his eyes fell upon on the young man standing in front of him. "Kim! Good you could come!"

Kim Lee stood in his usual well-worn shorts and t-shirt. "Hello Professor, your message said it was important? Why did you want to meet back here at the lighthouse so soon?"

Keleeigan grinned. "Why, to show you the fruition of our work."

Next to Kim a woman uncomfortably shifted from one high-heeled foot to another. "Fruition? How? We are a long way from testing."

Keleeigan glared at Trisia Swain. "Hardly. Or don't you

trust my work?"

Trisia shifted again in her heels. She was on her way for a fun night on the town when she received the Professor's message. She shivered as the wind blew up her blue minidress. "Professor you know that we both trust your work. It is why we agreed to join you on this project. And in secret I might add."

Keleeigan gestured for them to come inside. "Well don't just stand out there come on in. I know it is still a bit chilly after the sun sets. If we are lucky, a storm will soon follow."

Kim's eyebrow raised as he closed the door behind them. "A storm? Why would that be lucky?"

"Because my boy, a storm is what we need!"

"I don't follow you."

Keleeigan sat back down at one of the large lab tables then swiveled his chair around to face them. "Well you know we couldn't generate enough power to create a stable time-field, right?"

Trisia's eyes narrowed. "Professor is this going to take long? I had other plans for tonight."

Keleeigan laughed. "My dear it won't take long at all. If you would let me finish explaining."

Trisia's eyes lowered as they fixed on the ancient wood floor. "Sorry."

"No problem my dear. Now as I was saying, you know that the new power cell I developed wasn't quite powerful enough to open a temporal field right?"

Kim nodded. "Yes, and I thought you were going to build another?"

"Yes that was my original plan, but it will take months to build and test a new cell with these systems. You know how finicky they are."

"Yes we do, all too well." Trisia said sighing deeply. It was part of her job to try to get the systems to work together in harmony. A lot more difficult than anyone originally thought due to the intricacies of the self regenerating power cell. Having to run to the basement for each calibration on the large cell didn't make the job any easier.

"Well, I think I may have found a workaround, and it should expand the field as well."

"A workaround?" Kim said looking rather perplexed.

"Yes and it should be here soon."

"Be here soon? I still don't quite follow."

"Well we need a massive amount of power and I think I found a good source. It won't be enough for a two-way trip in this case, but it will allow testing of the theory and equipment."

Thunder boomed in the distance as the rain began to pelt against the windows. Trisia looked through the dirty glass and started moving towards the door. "Professor I am sorry but I don't have time for games, and I had plans for tonight. I need to head out before this storm gets any worse."

"But my dear this is what we need."

"You keep saying that, but we still don't know what you mean."

"You will." Keleeigan said as he punched a button opening a small door at the top of the lighthouse releasing a small weather balloon.

Kim pointed to the button. "Professor, what did you just do? I don't recognize that panel."

Keleeigan smiled. "Why I started our trip of course, don't worry this will work. I have no doubts." His words hung in the air for a microsecond before a large lighting bolt struck the weather balloon and traveled down its connecting wire to the power accumulator that Keleeigan had installed in place of the giant light. It glowed brightly as it reacted to the sudden power surge. "Okay here we go!"

Trisia's eyes widened, and she bolted for the door. "I am leaving!"

"You can't! The process has already begun!"

Trisia opened the door but just beyond it an energy field covered the exit. "What have you done?! I am getting out of here!" She yelled running to the window on the far side, her heels clicking loudly on the wood floor.

"That won't work, the field is covering the whole lighthouse."

"The whole building? But that is impossible! Our calculations indicated a small stable rip would require more than the power cell was capable of. Let alone a whole building." Kim said as he ran to the panel that showed the energy level rising and going higher than the gauge could reliably measure.

"It is possible, and I am proving it!" Keleeigan said as a light flashed and blew out under the increased load. Another panel sparked and exploded.

"Professor! You must abort this madness!" Trisia said waving her arms.

"I can't! It is too far along!" Keleeigan shouted as the building began to twist and tear as though it was made of putty. "Don't worry we are only jumping a day ahead."

"No!" Trisia shouted before she fell backwards sliding across the floor with the sudden lurch as the lighthouse surged with power flickering in and out of existence then disappearing entirely leaving only an empty hole where it once stood.

The lighthouse twisted and pulled inside the temporal field but managed to snap back into shape. Keleeigan held on to the table as all sorts of images flashed through his mind. Distant past, possible futures, but as soon as it all started it stopped. The lighthouse emerged from the temporal warp with a loud crash.

Kim sat down and shook his head. "What was that?"

"The temporal field must need an adjustment." Keleeigan said still holding on to the table. "Whew, what a ride."

"So where are we?"

"Not where, but when. Should only be one day ahead in time."

Trisia got to her feet and quickly walked to the door, eager to leave but when she got outside, nothing was as she expected it. "Um Professor, I think you had better get out here."

"What's the matter dear? Something happen to your car?"

"In a manner of speaking, it is not here."

"What do you mean? We only went ahead a day."

"I don't think so, I think we moved distance rather than time."

Keleeigan walked outside and looked at the landscape. The grass covered land stretched as far as he could see. "This is impossible, I didn't change the land coordinates, only the temporal. Yet, I don't see the coast line."

Kim sat down at one of the consoles and activated the mapping system. He tried several configurations, but they all returned the same error. "Professor I can't get a fix on any GPS satellites. It's like they don't exist."

Keleeigan walked quickly to check the screen Kim was

looking at. "Why you are right. I guess we jumped a lot farther into the future than I thought. And moved in physical location as well."

"Professor? Do you have binoculars? I think I see something in the distance," Trisia called.

"Yes, I will be right there." Keleeigan said as he grabbed his large binoculars from another table and joined Trisia outside. "Now what are you looking at?"

Trisia pointed to some spots in the distance. "Over there. I think they are moving. Cars perhaps?"

"Too slow to be cars. Not to mention too big to be seen at this distance." Keleeigan said raising the binoculars to his eyes. "Oh no! But this can't be! This is impossible, how could I have made such an error?!"

Kim ran to join them. "What do you see?"

Keleeigan passed him the binoculars. "Here take a look for yourself."

Kim focused the binoculars and gasped. "Dinosaurs!"

Keleeigan sighed. "Yes, dinosaurs."

Trisia blinked. "How? I thought you said we were going into the future?"

"I don't know my dear, I don't know. It would seem that we have gone far into the past, back before this was coastline. So we didn't move in position as I thought, only time. But a lot more than I wanted."

"Professor I hate to say this, but I think they are coming this way," Kim said still looking through the binoculars.

"Yes I suspect they will. And more will join."

"Why?"

"Because my boy, dinosaurs like temporal energy. They are attracted to it for some odd reason."

"And how do you know this?" Trisia glared at Keleeigan.

"From a friend."

"And how did this friend know?"

"Never mind, let's just say I am sure she knew what she was talking about."

"We need to get out of here." Kim said finally lowering the binoculars. "They will be here soon."

"I agree, but we need lightning for a stable temporal field. And I don't think that is likely to happen any time soon," Keleeigan said gesturing to the bright sunny day, "do you?"

"No, but we can't just sit here!" Trisia said.

Keleeigan turned to go back inside. "Nor will we. I have an idea."

"I hope it is a good one," Kim muttered under his breath.

"It is, close that door Trisia."

"Why? That won't keep them out."

"No, but a force field will."

"Force field? Are you joking?"

"Hardly, if I adjust the harmonics of the field generator that I used to produce the temporal effect it should feel like a brick wall."

"How long will it last?"

"Should give us plenty of time, enough to wait for a nice lighting bolt."

"But even if we do, how will we get back home? You still don't know why we are here in the first place."

"Oh I will find out, trust me."

Keleeigan checked several circuit boards inside the temporal guidance system as another dinosaur slammed into their makeshift shield.

"Why don't they give up?" Trisia sighed as she looked out the window. Another raptor had joined the others, making six raptors and one Tyrannosaurus rex circling outside.

"That field while protecting us, also attracts them. A double-edged sword. And I think I found the problem." Keleeigan said producing a small burnt chip from deep inside the guidance system. "It looks like this chip fried locking us on to several million years ago instead of a day into the future. Very strange considering nothing else is damaged in the system."

Trisia glared at him. "Can you fix it?"

"Sort of."

"What do you mean 'sort of'?"

"Well I don't have a lot of spare parts here. A few yes, but this is a very delicate chip with an intricate clock. I can bypass it, but I don't know what will happen then. We could end up in an even worse position."

"We may not have a choice," Kim said emerging from the basement. "I double-checked the power cell, it is down to 76% and dropping fast. I don't think we have more than a few hours before the shield gives out."

Keleeigan nodded. "Yes based on the current drain, we have about four hours left. I didn't count on the dinosaurs constantly attacking the shield. It is draining much faster than I anticipated."

"Then what do we do?"

"We try to jump as soon as I bypass this chip."

"Now? I thought you needed a lightning strike?" Kim said.

"Wait a second! You said that if you bypass that we will have no way of knowing where we are going!" Trisia said running over to grab Keleeigan's arm.

"My dear, if we don't try we will be dino dinner. Would you prefer that outcome?"

"No! Of course not!"

"Then let go of my arm so I can finish this!"

"Sorry professor." Trisia said releasing his arm looking embarrassed. "But what about the power level? You said we needed lightning?"

"Well we needed that boost to stabilize and exit, not enter the temporal field."

"Well at least we can enter … wait … if we can only enter that sounds like we will be trapped?"

"We could be. It is only a theory of mine. And I hope I am wrong."

Kim frowned. "Professor, most of your theories are proven true."

Keleeigan sighed. "I know. But what other choice do we have?"

The shield shimmered as the Tyrannosaurus bashed into it again. "Professor the power dropped to 72%, how much do we need to make the jump?"

"If it gets below 70% we won't have enough to try." He said activating a program before he stood and walked across the room. "I need to check the power accumulator upstairs. Be right back." Keleeigan said as he started to climb the winding steps. A moment later he reached the top and pulled a small pocket video recorder from his lab coat that transmitted directly to his system below.

James looked out on the vast city and smiled as another hover car whizzed by their apartment. The sudden breeze flipped open the edge of his suit jacket. Red had asked if he wanted to see the future, the future they saved. And this was the result. Wars finally ended, humanity entering a golden age, power available for all. It wasn't Utopia, but it was certainly better than any other time period he had been to. And to think this used to be The Wasteland.

He and Red had taken an apartment and were relaxing for a while. Although she had encouraged him to embrace the current style that flattered his athletic build, he felt more comfortable in the same suit he wore during his days as an agent. Although truth be told, current style wasn't *that* much different. Atrus' cylinder beeped then his hologram flashed in front of James. "Sir, I am detecting a message from Professor Keleeigan."

James' eyes went wide. "Doc? How is that possible?"

"Well, before we left, he and I had a long conversation about the possibility of sending a data stream that given the right modulation, would have the ability, in theory, to create its own temporal signature pushing its way into–"

James rolled his eyes. "Never mind, what is the message?"

"Let me show you, it appears to have been made with a primitive 2D recording system." Atrus said as another projection appeared alongside him showing Keleeigan standing in a long white lab coat, his thinning hair a mess.

"James I hope you are receiving this. As Atrus no doubt has already told you, we did discuss the possibility of sending a special transmission that should punch through time creating a resonance in his matrix that could then be decoded into this message. At least that was the theory."

"Well I tried to," Atrus said.

"Atrus?"

"Yes Sir?"

"*Hush!*"

The professor looked back and continued. "This is only one-way communication, and hence a recording, or a message in a bottle if you will. I am sorry to be contacting you this way but I need your help. Well Red and you both.

"You see when Red escaped FBI headquarters I did manage to record a lot of data on her jump. I didn't know it at the time, as I thought all of my systems were fried beyond recognition, but one of the new data matrix survived, at least on some level. Not a lot, but enough.

"You may be asking, 'enough for what?' for TIME TRAVEL my boy! And I did it! It was wonderful! But there were unknown side effects, and to be honest I wasn't as ready as I thought. The main temporal calibration chip somehow failed and sent us back several million years. Dinosaurs are trying to break through as I talk. I managed to convert the temporal field into a rock hard shield. But the power drain is more than I anticipated. And these beasts aren't giving up.

I have just enough power to make one more jump. But sadly that is the wrinkle. While I have enough power to jump into the warp, I don't have enough to pull us back out again. I used lightning the first time to provide enough power to jump and then the power cell had enough to pull us back out. While the cell will regenerate given time, these beasts won't leave us alone long enough for it to do so. Of course even then it still wouldn't have enough power to pull us back out."

The professors image flickered. "I need to hurry, the power levels are dropping fast. I need you to get a replacement timing guidance chip from my lab. I also need you to bring your gun and its power cell. It is vastly smaller, but it is already calibrated and should be able to work in tandem with the one here. I have sent all the details to Atrus on a sub channel. I don't know where we will end up, and you two are the only ones that can help us. I have to go. I know time is relative but please hurry. Godspeed." The image froze, grew increasingly pixelated then dissolved piece by piece as though something failed *badly*.

"Atrus, did the data he sent come through?"

"Yes Sir, apparently he grew tired of the FBI and other aspects of the government, leading him to set up a new lab in secret. I have to coordinates and the entry codes. We should be able to get what he requires."

"Did he also give a date?"

"Yes, it is a year after we left him. I have enough information to give Red for a temporal fix."

Later they all met in the living room when Red returned. "I think the whole thing smells like a trap. The professor figured out how to travel through time? I don't believe it!" Red snorted.

"You already told me that you don't know how you do what you do. Who is to say if he couldn't figure out a way by watching you? And do you really think that he would try to trap you, *if* he could already travel through time himself? That doesn't make sense."

"Perhaps not to you, but it does to me. You haven't had people chase you trying to put you in a lab."

"True, but this is Doc, you know he wouldn't do that. And anyway can we take the risk that perhaps someone else could find his technology and change history with it? Doc wouldn't, but someone else?"

Red sighed. "You have a point. All right, we will go. But anything funny and we warp out of there. Deal?"

James grabbed, hugged, then kissed her deeply. "Deal my darling, deal."

Keleeigan quickly moved down the steps. "Power level?"

"71.5% and falling. I think if they hit three more times head-on it will be below 70%."

"All right get ready we are going to make another temporal transition." Keleeigan said as he sat down at his main control station. "Okay brace yourselves this is going to be a bit rough." He said punching a button to drop the shield and activate the jump sequence. The raw power shot up into the accumulator in the light area as a temporal bubble started to form then burst out just as Keleeigan grabbed the console.

The temporal energy enveloped the lighthouse growing in intensity then with a sudden lurch they were yanked from this world. The universe turned and twisted upon itself. Kim coughed and fell over spilling what remained of the lunch he had an hour earlier. Trisia lay on the floor holding her legs to her stomach, trying not to do the same. Keleeigan forced the terrible feelings back and adjusted the controls slightly. He hoped it was enough.

—3—

Lightning struck the earth opening a large fissure in its wake. Slowly the rip expanded into a diamond shaped hole in the very fabric of space and time. It fluctuated from blue to dark red as James emerged landing on the grass with a thud. Red appeared a second later right behind him. The warp folded in upon itself disappearing from existence.

Red quickly glanced around, then hoped up. "Where are we?"

James stood up and smiled. "You should know, you were driving."

"Well we should be at the temporal coordinates that Keleeigan gave, but I don't see a thing. Atrus?"

"Yes Red?" Atrus said as his hologram flashed into existence before them.

"Are we at the target?"

"Based on the local clock setting, yes. And the primitive satellites concur we are in the right location as well."

"But there is nothing here." James said waiving his arms around. "Atrus what exactly did Doc send on the second channel?"

"He gave the temporal coordinates for his new lab–"

"Was that all?"

"If you had let me finish, no he also gave security codes to enter the complex."

"Did he actually say where it was?"

"If you mean other than giving the coordinates, no he did not give any further data on its location."

"Great, in the middle of nowhere and without a map. Is there anything nearby? Or anything unusual?"

"Moment ... scanning." Atrus said his eyes closed as if in concentration. "I do detect signs of vehicles driving on this grass in the recent past but nothing more than that."

"Vehicles?" Red asked looking perplexed. "I don't see any road here."

"It does not appear to be a road, rather the tracks come from one direction and stop without any sign of turning."

"And where is that?"

"Approximately ten meters straight ahead of our current position."

"Hmm let's check that out," James said heading off. After a few moments they reached the area, but it looked the same as everywhere else. "I don't understand this. Doc wouldn't give us this location with nothing here."

"I agree," Red said, "there must be more than we are seeing."

James' eyes flashed with a thought. "Atrus what *exactly* did Doc say?"

"Just the coordinates and the security codes."

"Are you sure he didn't say anything else?"

"Nothing of consequence."

"Atrus! What did he say?"

"Well he did mention something about announcements were always key in any conversation. I just thought he sent extra data by mistake."

James smiled. "Not quite. That was another key."

Atrus cocked his head. "I am not sure I understand."

"Watch and learn Atrus." James took a deep breath and stated very loudly. "I am James Moknkin requesting access to this facility."

"I do not understand what–" Atrus started to say before the bottom dropped out. A large panel of ground suddenly rocketed down several hundred feet before stopping with a bone jarring jolt knocking them flat except for Atrus, his hologram flickered but continued to stand in the same position, his eyes wide.

"I think you do now though," James grunted as he stood up. Just off to the right a short tunnel extended into darkness. "After you," James said smiling at Red.

"Thank you love." Red said as they stepped off of the platform and into the corridor. The large lights embedded into the ceiling activated and a second later the platform whooshed back up to ground level. "Well I hope there is an easy way to get that back down here," Red said looking up.

"I am sure Doc left a call for it. Atrus do you find one?"

"Yes Sir I do, to the right. I am surprised I couldn't detect this from above. It is quite disconcerting that it could have avoided my scans."

"I wouldn't worry about it too much Atrus, I suspect Doc shielded it. Let's see where this goes."

At the end of the tunnel lay a thick steel door with a single keypad. "Ah, here we are." James said as he walked towards the keypad. After three steps twin red beams flashed out from either side of the door and locked on both of them.

"Okay genius, now what?" Red said glaring.

"Improper voice print. Please state name and authorization code on keypad or termination system will engage."

"Unusual Professor Keleeigan would go through this much security for his lab don't you think?" Atrus inquired.

"Improper response. Please state name and authorization code."

"Shhh. I am James Moknkin please verify."

"Verification complete. James Moknkin is authorized, please enter code in sixty seconds or firing sequence will commence."

"Holy! Atrus, what was the code he gave you?"

"49242 Bravo Sirius Omega." Atrus said as James entered the code on the small keyboard.

"Authorization accepted, please stand back from the door." The voice boomed. The sound of metal on metal grinding could be heard as if large pins encircling the door were being withdrawn. The large circular door slowly ratcheted open then swung out of the way. "Welcome James Moknkin." Lights inside flickered to life revealing a very large area carved from solid rock. Along the furthest wall large rack servers sat with blinking status lights as various programs continued to run. Many work tables lined the lab containing an array of projects while others held only new ready-to-use components. Along another wall a containment unit with a full HASMAT suit hung on a hook next to the door. In the corner a shielded area with 'Danger High Voltage' labeled clearly above it.

"Wow Doc did move everything here from his main lab. I recognize most of this equipment."

Atrus appeared before them. "I am surprised he managed to relocate with all of his equipment. Based on what I know of your government, wouldn't the FBI director inform him this is all government property? Or give some sort of statement about national security?"

James smiled. "Atrus, Doc has a lot of friends in very high places. And I suspect he paid for all of this himself anyway. They couldn't keep it, well they probably tried, and he made a few calls and they were stopped dead in their tracks."

"I see," Atrus stated.

"What are we looking for?" Red said as she looked around the large room.

"Some sort of chip. Not sure where it is though. Atrus, did Doc say where it is?"

Atrus shook his head. "I am afraid not."

"Great a needle in a haystack hunt."

Suddenly the large screen on the wall flashed to life with Keleeigan's face. "James if you are seeing this message it is because something has gone very wrong with my latest experiment: Time Travel. You may be wondering why the new lab? When I located a small portion of data on Red's jump that had not been destroyed, I found myself watched even more than usual. And it was a bunch of little things here and there that added up to someone with connections wanted my discovery, but held back as they couldn't figure it out on their own.

"Every time I felt like I was getting close, I hit another brick wall. My servers were hacked several times, I didn't report it because I didn't want the FBI knowing for sure that not all the data was lost. The hacker couldn't get far enough in to retrieve anything, but that they got in at all is shocking. And they covered their tracks too well, I couldn't tell if it was the government or some other faction. But I suspect it was our own government trying to keep tabs on me. Heck when I say government I mean Director Ridblam. He has had it in for me for some time, even before I helped you save the president.

"It got to the point where I couldn't sneeze without an agent wiping my nose. I knew sooner or later that they were going to figure it out. Temporal fields are not exactly easy to hide anyway. So I got out of there and set up this lab. And created a new larger power cell similar to the one in your gun. But I couldn't quite create a stable temporal field. I still didn't have enough power, at least not enough to properly enter and exit a temporal field. Then I remembered this old lighthouse I had in New Hampshire. I figured that if I reworked the lamp area into a power accumulator, then captured a lightning bolt it should be enough power to not only open a stable temporal field but create one large enough to take the whole lighthouse with it. Crazy perhaps, but I had to try it.

"Unfortunately if you are seeing this, it means that something has gone very wrong and I need your help. I can't say what went wrong at this point, but I hope you already know. The computer to the right of this screen has an inventory of everything in the lab, and its location. It should help you locate whatever I told you to get. Or at least I hope it was me, otherwise … never mind. I know I can count on you both." Keleeigan said smiling before the image winked out.

"Atrus can you access the computer he indicated?" Red said turning to face him.

"Does a cat have fur?" Atrus said smiling.

Red's eyes narrowed. "Atrus just answer the–"

"Sorry Red, I see my attempt at humor has failed. Yes I can and have already done so. The chip should be located two tables over from here and one up."

James walked over creating echos on the concrete floor. "Which chip? I see several here."

"While there isn't a photo, the description says a rectangular chip with an extension on the one side."

"Ah here it is." James said reaching for it.

"Wait! Most of such components are very static sensitive. As a precaution, I suggest using the gloves on the far corner of the table and place it in of the ESD protected boxes to the left of the gloves."

"Whoops! Thanks Atrus."

Atrus bowed. "You are welcome Sir."

Red continued to look around the lab. "His work is very impressive, especially for this time. But it seems that there are several new projects here that aren't mentioned in history."

James looked up after he placed the chip in its protective case. "Did you look up all of his accomplishments? Is it possible you missed one?"

Red shook her head. "Unlikely. Which means he never finished them."

James' eyes narrowed. "Are you saying we shouldn't help him because it is obvious we can't?"

"It does look that way from what we know so far."

"Isn't it possible that you don't know all of his accomplishments? Or that history has been altered and we are seeing the effect of that, and it is up to us to put things right?"

"I suppose, but it is not the feeling I have at the moment."

"Are you opposed to us trying?"

"I don't know," Red said with a shrug.

"Atrus, based on what we know so far. Is there any risk in attempting a rescue?"

Atrus closed his eyes as if in deep concentration. "I do not see any risks in addition to the usual ones when we jump. At this point I think the situation is manageable."

James smiled. "There you see? Shouldn't we at least try?"

"I wasn't saying we shouldn't. I just have a bad feeling about it is all." Red said walking over to loop her arm in James' then smiled. "Now let's go see if we can find Keleeigan."

— 4 —

The air began to swirl on the long forgotten plain. With a thunderous crack, lightning stuck the earth opening a rip in space and time which quickly grew in size until finally James crashed out onto the grass with Red right behind him. The warp flashed, grew a tiny amount, then shrank to a single point before disappearing.

Looking up James saw something shimmering some distance from them. "Is that Doc?"

Red squinted as she stood. "Could be. Atrus can you confirm?"

Atrus flashed in front of them. "Affirmative, it is indeed, I can also confirm several dinosaurs attacking."

"What are we waiting for? Let's go save Doc."

"Warning! I detect a strong temporal fluctuation."

James looked around. "Didn't the warp close properly?"

"Correct, this is from the lighthouse. Apparently Professor Keleeigan is attempting to jump."

"He can't! Not without this chip! I thought we would arrive before the jump?"

"It would seem that the temporal coordinates were off, or he sent them too late for us to arrive in time to reach him."

The air appeared to shimmer as the lighthouse grew

23

brighter.   A second later a blinding flash erupted, and it disappeared.   The Tyrannosaurus rex looked around perplexed as did the raptors.   "Red?   There must be something we can do? Can't we go back say half an hour and save him?"

"And intrude on our time-line?"   Red shook her head. "No way. It could create a temporal implosion. You know that. Besides, if we get here earlier than when he sent us the message, that is one heck of a paradox and we don't want to find out the result."

"There must be something?"

"It may be possible to track the temporal signature using Red's crystal. But we will need to open the warp as close as possible to the location where the lighthouse disappeared. And we will need to do it quickly before the signature fades."

Red looked towards Atrus aghast. "Are you insane? We can't do that, there are dinosaurs all over the location. We would be a meal!"

James pointed. "Ohhh Shoot! Red I don't think we have a choice! They see us!" James said as the huge Tyrannosaurus rex ran for them.

"I hope the gun has a full charge!" Red shouted.

"It does but you know what happened last time. It didn't stop him unless I used full power."

"If I may make a suggestion. An energy blast on a certain frequency should freeze them in place giving us the time we require," Atrus stated.

"I tried stun blasts before and it did nothing but make them angry." James said whipping out the gun. "What is the frequency?"

"One moment I am scanning them."

"Atrus hurry!" Red said lowering herself, getting ready to run. The Tyrannosaurus rex would be upon them in seconds.

"I have a lock, the proper frequency has been entered into the weapon. Fire when ready."

"Okay, I have him in my sights …wait …you already configured it? How?"

"May I suggest we discuss this later?" Atrus said with an element of fear in his voice.

James nodded and pulled the trigger. A cone of light blue energy erupted from the barrel enveloping the Tyrannosaurus just as he reached them. He bent down, his jaws open, when he froze and stayed there. As if someone pushed pause on an old movie. The smaller raptors behind him were also simply standing there. "Wow it worked. How long will that last?"

"I am not certain, speed is of the essence," Atrus replied.

Red nodded and ran down to where the lighthouse stood. A few minutes later James arrived. "Okay now what?" James said breathing hard.

"Red give James the crystal and hold it next to me," Atrus said.

James took the crystal and held it next to Atrus' cylinder. "Okay now what?"

"I am scanning the very faint temporal signature. I have a lock coordinates are 30.0167N, 31.2167E temporal location 2545 BC."

James' eyes went wide as he handed the crystal back to Red. "That is Giza in ancient Egypt. Are you sure?"

Atrus nodded. "Quite sure. Now if I may suggest we jump as quickly as possible? I detect the paralyzing effect on the dinosaurs is starting to wear off."

"Red, can you do a jump this quick? Or do we need to find a place to rest for a while?"

"I think I am okay."

"Are you sure? And how many jumps will this take to get there?"

"I think we can do it with one jump."

"One? I thought it would take several being so far ahead of us?"

Red nodded. "Normally yes but with the crystal, it should be *just* within my range." She lowered herself in a sprinting position. "Ready?"

James smiled "You know it!"

Red bolted, and the air started to swirl. A moment later lightning struck opening the warp. Several dinosaurs started moving shaking their heads. But the warp started to shrink instead of grow.

"Red the dinosaurs are starting to move, we need to go now! What is wrong?"

"More tired than I thought. And the warp is taking more energy than usual. I need to stop."

The Tyrannosaurus lowered its head, let out an ear-shattering roar, turned around, and ran for them at full speed. "Red hang on! Don't stop!"

"But I have to! Too tired." By now the warp had shrunk to only a few inches in size.

"I should have done this in the first place." James muttered quickly reconfiguring the gun and raised it up, smiling. "Eat this you over grown iguana," James said pulling the trigger.

A massive blast of sonic energy erupted from the weapon hitting the Tyrannosaurus rex head-on freezing him in his tracks then he began to come apart as the energy enveloped him exploding every one of his cells in the same instant. The blast wave radiated out and spread to the nearby raptors. They let out a final roar before disappearing from existence. "There, that got 'em."

"James! No! You promised!" Red squealed as her speed doubled, then quadrupled before a sonic boom erupted in her wake causing the warp to quickly expand enough to drive a truck through then started to shrink as Red's speed started to fade again. "Yoooou *promised!*"

"Later! We have to go! *Now!*" James said pointing to the shrinking rip in time.

"Go!" She shouted as James jumped in and she followed right after. The warp slammed shut with a thunderous crack that shook the ground for miles.

"Professor, I don't think we are in Kansas anymore," Trisia said wide-eyed.

"What do you mean? We never were in Kansas!"

"Well, umm come look." She said pointing out the doorway. The temporal energy field continued to shimmer just beyond it, blocking the exit.

Keleeigan walked over and gazed out at the sand and the enormous mountain of stone that formed a pyramid shape in the distance. "It would appear that the temporal matrix is more unstable than I thought as we traveled a great distance as well as time."

"We are in Egypt!" Kim exclaimed.

"Not just Egypt, ancient Egypt about 2545 BC I should think judging by the Great Pyramid finished and the next one under construction. That makes this the reign of Khafre, one of Egypt's most tyrannical pharaohs from the old kingdom. Although they didn't call them pharaohs back then."

"Oh no! Look! I see someone walking, they will surely spot us and we will alter history!" Kim said as he pointed to a worker walking across the sand. The man wore a short square of fabric wrapped around his waist and walked across the sand barefoot. He seemed to pause for a moment to look in their direction, then continued on his way. "Hmm you would think they saw a lighthouse every day."

"I suspect we haven't emerged from the temporal field quite enough to actually be seen."

Trisia's eyes widened further. "You mean we aren't actually here?"

"Oh we are most certainly here. But they can't see us. And this is very bad."

"Why? We made it here, can't you just give us a boost and emerge when the power cell recharges?" Kim asked as he turned to face the Professor.

Keleeigan sighed as his eyes drifted down. "No."

"Why not?"

"Because the power cell is fighting to maintain this field. And if I shut it down, we will be forced back into the warp."

"Isn't that good? We could head back home."

Keleeigan shook his head. "No no, you don't understand. Based on my research, we would be trapped in the warp … forever. The power cell will never be able to pull us back out if we shut down now. Thankfully it takes less to maintain the temporal field than it did to create it in the first place. Sort of temporal inertia, but the power system is fighting a losing battle. It will give out and soon. Then we will have no hope of exiting let alone returning to our own time."

"Professor I think we have an even bigger problem." Kim said as he looked over several consoles. "If I am reading this right, the field is also very unstable it could shift at any moment."

Keleeigan walked over and checked the various instruments several times on the console. "You are right. I sure hope they can find us before we slip back into the warp."

"Who?" Trisia asked as a panel sparked than another before the whole building shook.

"No time! We are jumping! Hang on!" Keleeigan said before the view of Egypt with its Great Pyramid disappeared being replaced by a large wall.

The sun shown down with its intense glare. The day was a normal summer scorcher as the wind began to pick up and sand started to swirl as lightning reigned down hitting the hard ground with a thunderous crack leaving a red ragged gash in the very fabric of space and time. It oscillated, flashing several colors before suddenly expanding many times its size. James fell out with a large thud with Red landing right behind him. The warp flashed, grew several times its normal size, then slammed shut vanishing from existence.

"Remind me to kill you later," Red mumbled weakly.

James crawled over to her. "I am sorry love, I had to. We didn't have any choice."

"But you *promised!*"

"I know love, I know," he said kissing her softly, "and I am sorry."

"I am still going to get you later." Red said weakly then smiled. "But need to rest now."

"Yes love you rest. I will take care of everything."

"You had better." She said squeezing his arm, a second later she was fast sleep upon the hot sand.

James stood up. "Atrus, where are we?"

Atrus flashed in front of him. "I thought the giant gleaming structure to your left would be a good indication."

James looked up at the giant pyramid and snorted. "Of course I know that. I was asking for more details. And do you detect Doc in the vicinity?"

"I see. Well we are on the Giza Plateau and while I can't be certain, we are in the general vicinity of our intended target time-zone based on the completed pyramid to your left and the slightly smaller unfinished one to your right. I should be able to get a more exact time frame tonight via a star fix."

"How is it you were able to tell exactly when Doc landed but not if we are there?"

"The warp's temporal field was fluctuating more than I am used to, I cannot be certain other than a vague approximation. Red may be able to tell you more when she wakes."

"Great. So we need to keep out of sight and try not fry in this heat." James said as a bead of sweat ran down his cheek.

"I do detect a local approaching in the distance."

"Great more bad news. Neither of us look like ancient Egyptians."

"Sir, if I may, I think I can help with that."

"How?"

"By projecting the bottom of the pyramid a meter or so in front of us. Unless he tries to actually touch it, the effect should be convincing."

"Do it and hurry!"

"Acknowledged, activating projection." Atrus whispered as a sloped, gleaming, limestone wall appeared in front of them. Then the back became translucent allowing James to see the man who came into view as he turned the corner of the pyramid. He was barefoot and wore a white tubular piece of fabric around his waist like a kilt. The man looked around as if perplexed. Obviously he heard something, or thought he did. He walked several meters along Atrus' projection, shrugged his shoulders and turned back around leaving the way he came.

When the man was well out of sight James finally dared to breathe. "Whew that was close. Nice idea Atrus. But we are still lacking the proper clothing for this time."

"Yes, I agree that is a problem. But I do have another suggestion."

"Which is?" James said peeking around the corner of the pyramid making sure the man wasn't returning.

"I give you clothing for the proper time."

James' eyes opened wide. "Since when can you replicate matter?"

"I cannot, although I do have a theory where I might be able to create items using–"

"Atrus?"

"Sorry Sir. While I cannot replicate matter, I can generate a holographic field around you appearing as if you are wearing the proper clothing."

"And that will work? Are you sure?"

"The theory is sound; however, there will be limitations."

"Such as?"

"Well the largest one being, rapid movements may allow you to shift outside of the holographic clothing. I can only scan your nervous system so fast, there will be a slight delay between what I see and can respond to. In normal situations it will not be noticed, but if you move quickly, the projection may not keep up."

James smiled. "I think I can live with that. Do it."

Atrus nodded. "Acknowledged, activating projection."

A moment later James stood naked with the exception of what the previous man wore: a white kilt. "Atrus? What is with the kilt? Can't I have something else?"

"I am sorry Sir, but that is the current style and will remain so for hundreds of years. And it is called a *shendyt* not a kilt."

"And what is the difference?"

Atrus looked as if in deep thought for a moment. "None that I am aware of."

James snorted. "Exactly my point. Now then do you have any idea where I can find some real clothes? And where I can put Red for now?"

Atrus looked around. "I detect a small depression in the rock wall on the other side of the pyramid. Red should be safe there for the moment. But I suggest you activate the Shell to make sure. I can stun anyone should they get too close."

"Good idea," James said as they walked along the base. A few minutes later they found the depression. James carefully placed Red in the small area. It was a tight fit but not too bad, and it would keep her out of the sun. He unzipped her body suit along the legs and her chest to allow for some air cooling, then placed her backpack in her lap. Removing the cone-shaped Shell from his backpack he activated it and placed it on her lap as well. He then reached through the hologram and took off his already very moist jacket, shirt and pants placing them in his pack. He put the gun and its holster back on, then slipped Atrus into its small extra pocket on the side causing the holographic clothing to flicker again. As he turned to leave Atrus spoke.

"Sir, I suggest you leave your backpack here with Red as well."

"Why? I might need what is in it."

"Because it is difficult to maintain a believable image with such a large bulge on your back. I can do it, but I need to make you look far more muscular than you are. And the image movement accuracy may degrade further."

"Meaning my arms may show through the image even moving slowly?"

Atrus nodded. "Correct."

"All right. I will leave it here." He placed it in Red's lap under the Shell, then turned the Shell so its translucent spherical end faced outward. "And Atrus, can you project a hologram through the Shell to make this wall look as though it is solid?"

"Yes but it will consume extra power from the Shell that might be needed later. I do not understand why you would want me to do so?"

"Because she might be seen from a distance, but if nothing is here, there is less chance of someone wanting to investigate."

"You are quite correct. Impressive show of logic Sir."

James nodded and mimicked Atrus' usual bowing movement. "Why thank you."

Atrus' eyes narrowed as he activated the hologram making Red disappear from sight. "I got your point, that wasn't necessary."

James laughed. "Oh I thought it was."

James walked for some distance along the large wall still sweating profusely even after removing most of his real clothes. "How much farther is it?"

"The funerary temple is just ahead. From there we can exit and head west."

"West? Why west?"

"The mortuary complex is located there. Some of the tombs should yield the clothing you require."

James' eyes widened. "Grave rob? I am not going to rob a tomb. And wouldn't it affect the time-line?"

"Sir may I remind you that the tombs were robbed later

on anyway, doing it earlier will not change the time-line significantly, if at all. And at the moment, I do not see an alternative."

James sighed. "You are right. If we take them from anywhere else, they are going to be missed quickly. If I recall, unless you were very rich, one did not have a lot of clothing."

"Correct."

"Ah here we are." James said standing outside of a slightly hidden passageway cut into the wall.

"Yes, and if I may make another suggestion, activate your A.T.E.?"

"What? That automatic translator? It didn't work. And anyway I didn't bring it."

"Autonomous Translating Earpiece. And I think I have found a way to improve its accuracy."

"What good is that since I didn't bring it."

"Sir, feel your right ear. It is there."

James reached up and felt the small nub inside his ear canal. "Oh I forgot I still had it in. All right, what do you want me to do?"

"First turn on the device and put me into direct physical contact so that I may upload the update."

"Okay." James said reaching through the hologram, removing Atrus' cylinder from his holster, the A.T.E. from his ear, and let them touch.

"Upload complete. Since both units share the same matrix on a sub channel, it will work for Red's as well. You can replace the A.T.E. and me."

James nodded placing the A.T.E. back into his ear and Atrus' cylinder into his holster. "Okay now what?"

"It may take a little time monitoring a language to build up the translation matrix, but afterwards the translation should be instantaneous."

"Why doesn't that give me confidence?" James said as he entered the back of the temple.

"I have no idea," Atrus whispered.

Exiting the corridor at the back of the temple revealed several people giving offerings to the various statues that surrounded the courtyard. James huddled against a wall and whispered. "Atrus, what do you suggest?"

"That you walk into the courtyard, turn left and exit the building. Then turn right to head west and to the minor tombs we require."

"You make it sound so easy."

"Because it is Sir. Trust me. They will not see anything unusual."

"I hope so." James said as he took a deep breath and started walking. Thankfully Atrus was right, no one looked at him twice. A few glanced in his direction for a moment then continued what they were doing. Fifteen minutes later he exited the temple and was on his way toward the smaller tombs. By now the sun was lower in the sky and the air was not quite as oppressive.

"Atrus? I don't think the translator is working, I still didn't hear anything close to English."

"Sir, I told you it would take some time. But once completed the translation should be instant, allowing you to have an active conversation."

"I hope we won't need it. My plan is to find Doc and get him back to our time-zone."

"A good plan Sir; however, isn't it also wise to have a backup plan?"

"True, but I would prefer we don't need it."

"Yes. However, you just admitted we should have one."

James sighed. "Yes Atrus you are right."

"Thank you, Sir."

James rolled his eyes. "Okay, I see the tombs in the distance but which one do we want?"

"The ones closest to the Great Pyramid are the newest, best candidates."

"All right." James said as they finally approached one of the small rock buildings and stood in front of it. "Now what? I don't see a door."

"It is two steps to your right. The release is three depressions to the right and up from there."

"And what do I do? I assume there is a trick?"

"If you mean turning both symbols of the cartouche near the deceased's name so that they face the Great Pyramid a trick, then yes I suppose it would fit that description."

James rolled his eyes again. "Well why didn't you just say so?"

"I thought I did?"

"Never mind," James said as he turned both stone shapes and he heard what sounded like grinding then a strong click. "Did that do it?"

"Yes, I detect the door is unlocked and the traps have been disabled. Simply push the wall front of you and the hidden door should slide open."

James pushed, and the door slid with ease revealing a dark inner chamber. "Kind of dark, where is the light switch?" James joked.

"Allow me." Atrus said as he projected a bright light revealing the chamber to be filled with items. In the center lay a brightly painted stone sarcophagus. Chairs, chests, small and medium-sized statues filled most of the area. With jars placed in many recesses cut into the stone building.

"Okay, which one holds what we are looking for?"

Atrus appeared and pointed to an ornate chest. "It would appear that this one holds what you require. And the one to the right holds clothing for Red."

James opened the chest and saw mostly white skirts. "Are you sure this isn't for Red? I only see white skirts."

"As I said before, these items are what men of this time period wore. And they are called *shendyt*, not skirts."

"All right all right, *shendyt* it is." James said removing one of them and then taking its matching cloak. "At least with this my shoulders and back won't get burned." Opening the second chest revealed several long form fitting dresses. "I wonder why this guy had dresses buried with him?"

"According to the inscriptions on the chest, they are to be given to his wife in the afterlife as a surprise."

James raised an eyebrow. "Interesting, that would be quite the surprise I suppose."

Atrus nodded. "Indeed."

Atrus deactivated James' projection as he moved the gun holster to his inner thigh and wrapped the shendyt around his waist as instructed, then set the cloak on his shoulders. "Okay one problem, how do I get this dress to Red without tipping off everyone in that temple? Is there another way back to her?"

Atrus shook his head. "I am afraid not. However, if you roll up the dress and hold the fabric close to you, I can hide it holographically."

"I thought you said you couldn't hide my backpack that way?"

"I didn't say I couldn't, I said it would be more difficult.

And this dress is far thinner if you roll it up. I should have no problem disguising it. I also suggest taking the thin linen bag next to the dress."

"What's that for?"

"It appears to be a gift bag for the dress itself."

"And why do I need it?"

"It will be useful to disguise your backpacks. It is also thin and easy to hide with the dress."

"All right, let's get out of here before someone spots us." James said as he closed the two chests, carefully resealed the door to the tomb, and made his way back to Red.

Some time later James reached the temple. He walked towards the back but was stopped several times by various people greeting him. He smiled and greeted them in return. Once inside the pyramid wall he risked talking to Atrus. "What was all that about?"

"I do not know, they did seem more interested in you than last time."

"They sure did. Before no one said boo, this time they all wanted to stop and greet me. And I thought you said the A.T.E. would improve? I barely understood what they were talking about. If it wasn't for their slight bowing gesture, I would not have guessed."

"It will. It just needs more of a language sample."

"I certainly hope so. And are you sure Red is still all right? I don't see her." James said as he continued to walk along the enclosure wall.

"Yes. She is still in the same location and has not moved. I cannot tell you if her condition has improved or not without a close intensive scan."

"Where is she again? I thought she was closer than this."

"Approximately fifty meters ahead. I will disable the

hologram when we get closer and can verify no one is in the area."

By this time the sun had almost set, and the air had become cooler. When James reached the location, the hologram dissolved revealing Red just as he left her. He leaned down and touched her shoulder. "Red? Are you okay?"

"Mmm?"

"Please wake up. You can sleep later."

Red's eyes fluttered open. "Why can't I sleep now?"

"Because this is too exposed. I got you some clothes." James said as he passed her the dress.

Red's eyes finally focused on what James was wearing and whistled. "Nice legs."

"Oh hush you," he said helping her to her feet.

Red grinned. "Never thought I would see you in a skirt."

"It is a *shendyt* not a skirt."

Atrus appeared before them. "That is quite correct."

Red rolled her eyes. "Picky picky." Then unrolled the dress holding it up. It was a basic tube shape with two straps that went up around the neck. "Is this all you could find?"

"I'm afraid so. But from what Atrus tells me, this is what the fashionable females are wearing for most of the ancient Egyptian period."

"Well looks like for once I have the better end of the deal in the clothing department." Red said as she started to slip out of her bodysuit and into the dress. But she frowned when she finished. The straps did go up and around her neck but the dress itself barely covered her breasts. "You would think you could get my size right."

"I didn't have much choice!"

"Red, it is actually the style of the dress not the size," Atrus said before his image winked out.

"Atrus? Is someone coming?" James asked looking around.

"No. No one is approaching. My power level is currently running low due to all the extended holographic projections today, and I must conserve what is left in case you need me."

Red snorted. "Not the size? I highly doubt that, and before you say anything Atrus, you are a man so no I don't believe you either."

"Red I am not–"

James shook his head. "Atrus?"

"Yes Sir?"

"Trust me, let it go."

"I do not understand, but acknowledged."

"Red, do you know where we are?"

Red looked up as she slipped into the sandals and fastened the belt around her waist. "Ancient Egypt-based on the big pyramid there and these clothes."

"Very funny. You know exactly what I meant."

Red chuckled. "Yes, but you know I had to," She said slipping him a kiss.

James smiled. "I know. Now where is Doc? Atrus said he didn't pick up his temporal signature. Are we off course?"

"No, this time I altered our exit point. We should be anywhere from a day to a couple of weeks ahead of him. That should give us time to get the lay of the land and be better prepared."

"Good idea. So what's our next move?"

"Well," Red said watching the sun slip below the horizon. "I am sure with the sun down it is going to get cold out here. We should find shelter. Not to mention being next to the pyramid at night may not be a good idea. We don't want to be mistaken for tomb robbers."

James eyes drifted up then darted back. "Right. Any ideas? Have you been here before?"

"No, I never traveled to ancient Egypt for some reason. But based on Khafre's pyramid is still under construction, the builders city would be our closest bet. If I recall correctly, it was south of our position. Atrus can you verify?"

"Yes Red, such a settlement does exist to the south. I can project it if you like."

"Do you have the power?"

"Yes, a short projection should not be an issue. Engaging holo system." An image of a decent sized town appeared in the air. Green dots indicated a lot of people in the settlement. By the one corner a guard house seemed to watch the only entrance.

"Atrus, is that entrance the only way in?" James said pointing to the guarded area.

"I am afraid so. It would appear that ancient Egyptians were very cautious with their state-run projects." Atrus said as the image winked out.

"Well, do we have any other choice?"

Red shook her head. "Not really, I think Saqqara, the next city is a few miles south or Memphis which is south and across the river."

Atrus pipped up. "Red is quite correct. And I would recommend against traveling that far at night. Therefore, the builder's settlement is the best option."

"Okay looks like we're a building couple." James grinned as he took Red's hand and headed towards the temple and the exit. As they walked, James wished he could wear his normal shoes. The sandals, while cooler, were nowhere near as comfortable. By the time they reached the temple it was empty, and no one noticed them leave.

A short while later they found themselves at the entrance of the builders city. Two guards holding spears and wearing a menacing expression stood at either side. "I sure hope the A.T.E.'s are working." James whispered out the one side of his mouth.

"They should be Sir, the people talking in the courtyard of the temple provided a lot of data for the matrix."

"Okay here goes." James sighed and took a step forward. "Hello, may we pass?"

The one guard turned towards the other. "Ao ou pe ajof? I couldn't quite understand erof, did you?"

The other guard shook his head. "No I don't. Sounded really weird though. I bet this noble is trying to test our reactions."

James tried again. "Sorry, may we pass?"

The one guard looked at James as his eyebrows met and his eyes narrowed. "Since when do nobles make requests of us? You command and we obey."

James smiled. "I was trying to be polite."

The other guard smiled. "You are not like any other nobles I have talked to. They are usually self-absorbed with little tolerance. Would it be possible for me to be transferred to your *nome*?"

"Perhaps. If you serve me well."

The man nodded. "I shall. But if I may ask, what brings you here?"

Red tapped James' back, and he nodded. "We are traveling on official business. However, it is late and we wish to spend the night here."

"You will have to speak with the building administrator. He is located at the end of the street."

James nodded and inclined his head slightly. "Thank you we will."

A few moments after they had walked past the guards and were well out of earshot Red kicked James. "What the heck was all that about?"

James shrugged. "I have no idea. It seemed like a better idea to go with it than fight them on it. And anyway I don't think they would have let us pass if I did."

"Why do they think we are nobles?"

"I suspect it is due to your current clothing. Status was displayed by the types of clothing worn. Even without jewelry, James' cloak seems to indicate a high level of status as most others would not wear it at this time otherwise. And Red's kalasiris probably indicates nobility by the long length," Atrus whispered.

"I just put it on to keep my shoulders from being sunburnt."

"Wait a minute, my what?!" Red exclaimed in hushed tones.

"Your kalasiris, the dress you are wearing," Atrus replied.

Red sighed. "Oh. Well since we probably can't find anything else without raising suspicion, we had better go along with it. But I don't like it."

"Why not? These clothes might get us access we never would have got otherwise," James said with a shrug.

"That's what I'm afraid of."

At the end of the street they found the building administrator in his office looking over several papyrus scrolls. He was in his fifties judging by the lines on his face and the several streaks of gray in his hair. He looked up rather surprised as he eyed them, gazing up and down. "Hello! I am Sethy, what brings you here?"

"We are traveling and would like to spend the night if that meets with your approval?"

Sethy stood smiling. "Two nobles are always welcome here. Although we can only offer the most meager of services. But rest assured we will do our best."

James smiled. "Of course, we would expect nothing less."

"Please use my house, it is next door. My son left earlier today with business in Memphis, he won't be back for a few days. You are welcome to use his room until he returns."

"Thank you that is most kind," James said smiling.

"Please," Sethy said gesturing towards the door, "you needn't wait for me. I have more work to do. But my wife, Nyla, will see to your needs." He quickly returned to his work writing on the papyrus scroll.

Red and James walked over to the adjacent building and found Nyla inside hard at work with the scent of fresh bread wafting through the air. "Hello, if you are looking for my husband Sethy, he is next door," she said pointing a flour coated finger.

James nodded. "Yes we know. We are traveling and he said we could use his son's room while he is away."

"Yes of course. Two nobles are always welcome in our house. I fear we do not have much to offer, certainly not to the level you are used to. But I can offer you fresh bread and beer."

Red smiled. "The bread would be wonderful thank you. But I think we would prefer water. We do not wish to impose."

Nyla cocked her head. "Impose? It is no imposition at all, we welcome you to our house, and all that is in it."

"Thank you. Then we will take some of that beer and retire for the night. It has been a long day."

Nyla nodded. "Of course." She offered a bread bowl, and a stoppered container.

"Thank you again," Red said taking them, "and which room?"

"Second door on the right," she said pointing.

"Good-night." James said as they headed off, walking down the short hallway. Once the bedroom door was closed, he leaned against it letting out a large sigh as he relaxed. "I am very glad we could play the part."

"I am not so sure." Red said sitting down on one of the two woven chairs.

James sat down the bag with their clothes and backpacks in the corner. "Atrus are we alone?" James whispered.

"That is correct, no one is outside the door or otherwise monitoring the conversation."

"Good, then activate recharge."

"But Sir, you may need further use of my services."

"James is right, your power is low right now and we are okay for the moment."

"All right, but may I check on you in two hours time?"

"Yes if you are that concerned. And if everything is okay, you deactivate and continue recharge. Clear?"

"Yes Sir. Activating timed recharge." Atrus said before an almost inaudible beep occurred indicating his system shutting down and a recharge in progress.

Red awoke to loud voices coming through the mud brick walls. "What do you mean he is coming here?!" Sethy shouted.

Siamun took a step back. "Just as I told you, the king is coming here today. I tried my best but apparently one of his priests has convinced him of our embezzlement."

"Embezzlement?! I have served him faithfully for years! How could he think that!"

"Father, I do not know. I told you I tried my best. Perhaps you should have delivered the report in person."

"I can't leave here! There is too much at stake! Yes we are behind but if I leave, then the problem will be even worse not better. Why could you not convince him? All the information was clear in that report!"

"I tried father, honestly I tried," Siamun said hanging his head.

"I am sorry my son, I know that you did your best. The fault was not yours. It is the fault of the jackals that have the king's ear!"

"Shhh please you will wake our guests," Nyla said gesturing for quiet.

"There will not be any quiet in this house until the king leaves," Sethy sighed.

The rest of the conversation Red could not quite make out. She walked over and shook James' shoulder. "Hey, wake up sleepy head."

James' eyes fluttered open. "Hmm? What time is it?" he said stretching.

"Time to get up. Now move!" She said in hushed tones.

"Why? What is wrong?"

"The king is arriving soon."

"The king? What king?"

"The king of Egypt, who do you think?" Red said rolling her eyes.

"Why?"

"Apparently they are behind and he is coming for an inspection."

"Well so what if he is? We are only here for a day or two until Doc appears."

"May I remind you that it might be more like a week or two?"

James smiled as he sat up. "I doubt you are that far off. Your accuracy has been impeccable since you got the crystal back."

"I know, but still. I have a bad feeling about this." Red said as she sat in the chair with enough force to make the webbing squeak.

"Well we could lie low and stay out of sight for today, until he leaves." James said as he pulled out Atrus and pressing the bottom he heard a slight beep as he reactivated. "Atrus? Status?"

"My systems are fully operational, and power level is at 98%."

"Good, now we may have a problem. The king is visiting Giza today."

"The king? To which king do you refer?"

"See?" James said gesturing towards the cylinder. "I am not the only one to wonder about that. Atrus, The king of Egypt."

"Acknowledged, and how is this a problem?"

Red shifted uncomfortably in her chair. "I just have a bad feeling about it."

James sat back down, took her hands in his, and looked into her eyes. "I am sure you are overreacting. All we need to do is lie low for a few days and find Doc when he arrives. Atrus will know when that happens."

"Affirmative. I will know the instant his unique temporal signature appears."

"See? Nothing to worry about," James said smiling.

"I hope you are right."

Far in the distance a large boat docked and a grand procession made their way to one of the temples. "I believe the king has arrived. I detect a sizable assembly of people going into one of the temples," Atrus said.

Red sighed. "Looks like it is show time."

James squeezed Red's hand. "Shall we at least go talk with our hosts and make sure?"

Red nodded. "Yes you are right, we should at least talk with them before we leave."

They left the room and found Nyla busy making bread in the kitchen. "Oh hello. I am sorry if we woke you. I had intended on letting you sleep."

James raised his hand. "No, that is quite all right, we needed to be up anyway. But what was all the discussion about?"

"Oh you didn't hear?"

"Not clearly."

"Well the king is arriving today."

"The king? Do you mean the pharaoh?"

"Pharaoh?" Nyla stopped kneading the dough and looked at James with a blank expression. "No, he is not bringing his house. And I can't imagine how he could."

"I see. Is there a problem?"

Nyla shrugged as she continued to knead the dough then placed it in a large bowl. "The project is behind and Sethy is worried. He tried to explain the situation in his report, but apparently some of the kings court disagree and thought a personal inspection is required."

"I see, well thank you for the use of the room, we must be going now."

"So soon? You are certainly welcome to stay another day or

two if you wish. Siamun won't mind staying in the barracks for a couple of days."

"No we couldn't do that. You have already been so kind. Thank you." James said as they opened the front door and left.

"Sir, in this time period *pharaoh* only refers to his house, or place where he lives. It is not until the New Kingdom where he is addressed as pharaoh." Atrus said when they were more than two buildings away.

"Ah, I see."

Red elbowed James in the ribs. "I told you!"

"Ooof! I know, I know, you were right okay?" he said rubbing his ribs.

The instant they reached the guard house someone shouted "Hold him!" Two large men jumped forward and held James in an iron grip. Red took a step back, but they didn't seem to be interested in her.

"What is wrong?" James said as he looked at both men as a third one ran up to him.

"The king wants to see you."

James looked into their eyes and didn't like what he saw. "I have no problem in seeing the king, in fact I was going to see him later today."

One of the guard's eyes narrowed. "Oh really? Well then you won't mind if we make sure you do." He said as they escorted him off to one of the large temples to the north of the builders city.

After a bit manhandling by the guards, James finally arrived at the center chamber of a large temple. In the middle of the large expanse a throne was placed and King Khafre sat upon it. "When I was told one of my nobles was visiting Giza, I became suspicious. Especially when it did not sound like anyone I knew. And now that I see you, I can say I do not know you. Who are you? And how dare you make false claims to be a noble of mine!"

"This has all been a misunderstanding. I never said I was one of your nobles."

"Then why do you wear the shendyt and cape of one!"

"I–"

"He is a thief!" A priest from the right side of Khafre stepped forward. "I know that cape! It is Manakhtuf's!"

Khafre leaned forward and turned to face the man. "Ankef, are you sure?"

Ankef lowered his eyes. "There can be no mistake my king, the cape was made special for him and sealed in his tomb. I should know, I was the one that sealed it!"

Khafre's eyes flared. "Tomb raider! There is nothing worse than to steal from the dead and deny them pleasures in the afterlife! You shall die by morning in the way we punish all those that disturb the dead! Take him away and return Manakhtuf's cape to his tomb where he can make use of it!"

Ankef bowed. "Of course my king." He then walked over to James and removed the cape from James' shoulders then spit in his face. "May the gods show you no mercy. I can assure you we won't." Several men marched forward grabbed James and moved him forcefully out of the temple.

A short while later Red found James in a mud brick building under guard. She gave them a pretty smile and flashed her eyes. "May I speak with the condemned?"

"Why would you want to associate yourself with him?"

"I did not know he robbed from the dead as I testified in front of the king. But I wish to know why."

"He is not talking, I can't see how you will get any more out of him."

Red smiled again. "May I at least try?"

The lead guard sighed with a wave of his hand. "Let her pass."

Red walked in and looked at James. "Well this is quite the mess you have got yourself into," she said in hushed tones.

"Red! Get out of here, I don't want them to think you are with me," he whispered.

"Don't worry they think I am here to try to find out more. And why didn't you tell me you robbed a tomb for these clothes?"

"Shhh! I didn't think it was that important and Atrus suggested it."

"I only did what you asked: found clothing you required."

"Atrus! Hush! At least they didn't find you. I assume you still have the gun as well?"

James looked around the corner. "Yes I do. They didn't search me. Must have thought the only thing I took was the cape. But I haven't had a chance to use it, they have been watching me like a hawk. What about the bag with our packs, the Shell, and all of our clothes? Did they get that?"

"No I hid it just as they grabbed you."

"You hid it? Where?"

"In a mud brick wall. There were a few loose bricks, and it made the perfect hiding place."

"Why didn't you hang on to it?"

"Because someone was getting themselves arrested, and I didn't want them to find all of our stuff!"

"No one told me what my sentence is, only that it would be done in the morning."

"The usual sentence for tomb robbers was death by impalement," Atrus said.

"What? Why didn't you tell me this before?"

"You didn't ask. Nor did I expect the plain clothing items you took to be identified so easily."

"I obviously need to get out of here. Think you can distract those guards." James said jerking a thumb towards the men at the entrance of the building watching him.

Red smiled. "Maybe, you think you can actually take them out without being seen?"

James grinned. "You just leave that to me."

Red snorted. "You aren't exactly on a roll at the moment."

"I know, I know, just see what you can do, okay?"

"All right, you just be ready."

"I hate to intrude but I detect Professor Keleeigan's temporal signature."

"Wonderful, where?" James asked.

"A short distance east of this position," Atrus replied.

"Okay, we need to hurry, a modern lighthouse is likely going to draw a lot of attention," Red whispered.

"No kidding? Ya think?"

Red grinned then slowly walked outside. A slight breeze was blowing and she let it catch the edge of her dress flipping it up past her knee. "Wow windy today isn't it?"

The men looked at her and smiled. One answered, "Yes it is," then a blue flash and all of them fell in a heap.

"Well that worked well," James said still braced holding the gun pointing in their direction, "but I hope you didn't show them too much."

Red grinned then winked. "Nope, the rest is only for you."

"I intend to take you up on that," James said as he walked forward and slipped her a kiss, "Atrus? Where is Doc?"

"To your right towards the pyramid."

"I don't see anything." James said squinting trying to see.

"He hasn't fully emerged from the temporal field."

"That is strange. He should have long before now. Only a few seconds after Atrus first picked him up," Red said.

"I concur, but from what I can ascertain, the temporal field may not be stable."

"Which means?" James asked.

Red held up her hands and shook her head. "Don't look at me, I haven't had that much experience with unstable warps."

"There are many possibilities. He may only be stuck due to a lack of power as he feared. But perhaps we can find a way to help him out."

"And if we don't?" James asked.

"Then he may slip back and be trapped forever."

"Red, go get our stuff and I will go to Doc's location. Perhaps Atrus can find a way to communicate with him."

"And what happens if someone sees you? You are a wanted man remember? Especially when these guys wake up." Red said nudging one of them with her foot.

"They will be out for most of the day. And don't worry they won't recognize me. Atrus show Red your new trick."

"What new tri–" Red blinked as James' features blurred and he became a totally different person.

"It is just a hologram projection on top of my body. And before you ask it isn't perfect, I can't move fast. But it will keep people from running after me."

"Okay, I will go get the bag. See you in a few." Red said slipping James a kiss before she bolted running fast for the builder's settlement.

James walked in the direction that Atrus had indicated and a moment after he reached it, Red had retrieved the bag and stood alongside him. He took another step, but still couldn't see anything in the area. "Careful Sir, do not intersect the field. I do not know what might happen."

James looked towards Red. "Did you get everything?"

"Yes, and no one saw me, which is even better," Red said patting the bag slung over her shoulder.

"Warning! I detect a fluctuation. The temporal field is expanding. Stand back," Atrus said as blinding flash went off reveling the shimmering lighthouse.

"Red! Do you see it?"

"Yes, but it still has not emerged from the field."

James walked around to the other side. "Red! Over here!"

She ran around the corner to see James pointing. "What is it?" She turned to look at the open doorway revealing Professor Keleeigan flanked by two younger people.

"Atrus deactivate the hologram! Doc! Are you all right? Can you hear me?" James said and while they saw Professor Keleeigan's mouth move they couldn't hear anything.

"The temporal field is blocking all wavelengths that effect sound transmission. Warning! I detect another fluctuation is imminent, this one is far larger than the last. I suggest moving back to a safer distance," Atrus said.

"No I am not leaving Doc!"

"James! We have no choice, if something happens to us, then who will help Keleeigan?"

James sighed. "You are right. I will find you Doc! I will!"

The shimmer effect grew in speed flashing faster and faster as if the field was spinning. It continued to build until the effect was moving so fast that everything was an absolute blur before a blinding burst of light and everything disappeared leaving only faint lines in the sand behind.

"Atrus? Where is he now?"

"Scanning–"

"Do you need Red's crystal?"

"Negative, the field instability is making his signature easier to track ... temporal coordinates 215 BC and physical coordinates are 40.2882N 116.0686E."

"And where is that?"

"Juyong Pass."

James rolled his eyes. "And what is that?"

"It is a well-known mountain range that is part of the Great Wall of China, and used by Qin Shi Huang, the first Chinese Emperor, which also fits with the temporal coordinates."

"We have to go to a well traveled path when the first Chinese Emperor built the Great Wall of China? Couldn't he have picked a more remote location?" James groaned.

Red gripped his shoulder. "We never thought it was going to be easy."

"No, but I didn't expect it to be this hard either."

— 6 —

"Professor! I think I see someone approaching our position."

"Ah probably someone just walking past." Keleeigan said as he bent over a console checking several readings.

"No, I don't think so," Kim said pointing, "he brought someone else over."

"Someone else? Can they actually see us?" Keleeigan said as he walked over to the doorway. "Why that is Red, but I don't recognize the man that is with her." But as Keleeigan blinked the man's features blurred, then dissolved into James' smiling face.

"It looks like he is shouting, but I can't hear anything," Trisia said.

"No, the temporal field is blocking all wavelengths that sound travels on, we are lucky they can even see us. James! Read my lips, you need to stabilize the field then get us the chip and power supply!" Keleeigan sighed. "It is no good, he doesn't understand."

The building began to shake causing a small glass bottle that had moved to the edge of a table to fall off and shatter on the floor. "What now?" Kim said dashing to one of the makeshift consoles.

Keleeigan looked up towards the light and the source of

the temporal field. "The field is fluctuating, we are jumping! Hold on!" He said as there was a blinding flash and everything outside of the door vanished leaving only the angry colors of the temporal warp.

The lighthouse shook as it was pulled from one side to the other of the warp. "How much longer?" Trisia shouted over the groan of the tortured building.

"Not much I hope, the structure can't take much more of this instability."

"Is there anything you can do?" Kim asked.

"I can try," Keleeigan said as he tried to get to his controls, but the moving floor slowed his progress. Finally he reached them and ran a few quick checks. "I can try sending a short burst of power into the field. But it is risky. It will take the power cell down further, and shorten the amount of time it can hold the field."

"Do it!" Kim said. "We can't take much more of this."

Keleeigan hit several buttons and the temporal field flashed again pushing them out of the warp. "Well at least that stopped our reckless movement through the warp."

"Yeah but talk about out of the frying pan and into the fire." Trisia said as she pointed towards the open doorway.

"What now?" Keleeigan said as he turned around then wished he didn't for there in the distance revealed a large wall, a garrison, and several oriental men marching.

"Do you know where we are?" Kim asked.

Keleeigan walked closer to the doorway to get a better look. "Well we seem to be in a valley, and based on that large wall, the construction, and clothing of the men marching there. I would say we are between 300-200 BC. But since that wall looks so new, probably 215 BC smack dab in the middle of the reign of Qin Shi Huang the first Chinese Emperor. They don't appear to see us yet, I hope Red and James can get to us in time."

The warp twisted under Red's control causing an exit to open. James crashed out on a patch of grass near a line of trees and looked around a microsecond before Red joined him. "Where are we now?" James said spitting dirt.

"As Atrus said, 215 BC," Red said standing up.

"I said where not when," James said with a wink.

"Near the Great Wall, I didn't think popping the middle of Juyong Pass was wise. If I recall correctly, there was a large garrison there at this point in time."

Atrus appeared before them. "You are quite correct, there is, if my scans are to be believed." Atrus said as he projected a large overlying map of the area.

James whistled. "That is a lot of men, are you sure we can't be spotted from here?"

Atrus shook his head. "No we are on the other side of one of the mountains that make up Juyong Pass."

"So now what do we do?" James asked.

"Try to blend in and find some clothing that fits this period. And *this* time, don't rob a tomb," Red said as she glared at James.

"Hey! It was Atrus' idea!"

"Oh sure, blame the computer," Atrus said his eyes rolling upward.

"And *now* you call yourself a computer? I take it I am never going to live this down?"

"*No.*" Red and Atrus said in unison.

"Great," James sighed, "well if you have any suggestions I am open to them."

Atrus closed his eyes for a moment. "I detect a settlement not far from here."

"What kind?"

"I believe it is a worker village. Probably the families of those that worked on the wall live there."

James started to sweat in the humid climate. "Well at least it is not winter. And we definitely need to find a new change of clothes. Any idea how many people are in the village now?"

"I cannot tell from this distance. Most of the village is outside of my scanning range."

"I will go with you, at least until you are closer. No reason for me to hang around here," Red said.

James nodded. "Agreed," he said giving her a squeeze then slipping a kiss on her soft cheek, "besides I rather have you with me."

Red grinned. "That, Mr. Moknkin is very mutual."

They made their way through the forest until Atrus flashed in front of them. "This is very strange, I detect no one in the settlement."

"I thought you said we were out of range."

"We were at the time, but the entire settlement is now well within my detection radius, yet no one is there. I advise extreme caution."

Red and James both nodded. "Agreed."

By the time they reached the outskirts, it was well past noon. "Atrus?" James whispered, "is the coast still clear?"

"Affirmative, there is no one there. In the buildings, or in the general vicinity as far as my scanners can detect."

"I will take a look, activate the hologram."

"Acknowledged," Atrus said as he dissolved and a new matrix flashed over James. A second later he was clothed in a black tunic with a red belt, and cotton shoes.

"You stay here," James whispered.

"Why? There is no one in there."

"Because you are my backup. If I get into trouble, you can get out of here and come back for me later."

Red sighed. "You have a point. Dang, I hate it when you are logical."

James smiled and slipped her a kiss. "Actually, you love me more when I am. Wish me luck."

"Good luck love," she said kissing him back.

James slowly walked down the main road that led into the settlement. Nothing moved. Looking closer all appeared to be intact. He went from house to house, everything was undisturbed. Almost as if they got up and left, never to return. Several pots with now moldy meals showed signs of being in the middle of preparation when …whatever happened …happened. The footprints in several houses were old as well, no one had been here in a long time.

"Atrus? Anything in the area?"

Atrus flashed on in front of him. "Negative. Still nothing in scanner range."

"All right might as well deactivate my hologram and let's go get Red."

A few minutes later James joined Red outside the settlement and explained what he had found.

"Nothing at all? It is if they all just got up and left?"

"Yes. Nothing is broken, so I don't think they were forced. Or at least they didn't put up a fight. And we can help ourselves to their clothes, they won't will be missed." James said as they walked along the center street then pointed to a building that was slightly larger than the others. "Let's check in there."

Red nodded and followed him in. Inside the modest rammed earth building they found the contents undisturbed like the rest. She opened a small chest in the corner of a room just off of the kitchen and found two long tunics. One in black and one in blue. And matching shoes. "Hey in here."

James ran in. "What did you find?"

"Something to help us blend in and keep Atrus from draining his reserves while we do it," she said tossing him the black tunic.

"Nice, this will work. It is very similar to the one I had on in the hologram."

Atrus flashed on in front of them. "Actually Sir, it is called a *Shenyi*."

"Thank you Mr. Encyclopedia."

Atrus bowed slightly. "Thank you Sir." Then his image winked out.

James grinned. "You know one of these days he is going to figure out that is not a compliment."

"I heard that!" Atrus said.

"I know you did," James said grinning more.

"Atrus, any signs of what happened here?"

Atrus flashed on again in front of them. "As you already know this area has been unused for some time. Several months judging by the decomposing food."

"That doesn't make sense."

"Perhaps they were relocated?" James asked.

"No, if that was the case, then they wouldn't have left all this stuff. The buildings sure, but these clothes are worth something. Not to mention the pots, and all the other items here. What would make them leave and never return?"

James' eyes grew wide. "Plague?"

"No Sherlock, there would be bodies everywhere."

James chuckled. "True. It doesn't make sense."

They continued to the far end of the town and Atrus flashed on in front of them. "I detect an odd anomaly along this road just outside of town."

"What kind of anomaly?"

"I am not certain as it is just in range. But I suspect it may be a depression with a lot of people in it."

"The people from this village?"

Atrus shrugged. "It is possible. I cannot confirm or deny."

"Well let's check it out."

"Perhaps we shouldn't," Red said.

James looked at her. "Why not?"

"I think we should count our blessings and get as far away from here as we can."

"Wouldn't it be in our best interest to know what happened to the people here? And if we should worry?"

"I'm already worried. That isn't going to change." Red frowned.

"All right, we won't go if you don't want to."

Red sighed. "No you are right, we should know what happened here. Atrus keep your scanners peeled, I want to know if there is so much of a blip in the area."

"Acknowledged," he said before disappearing.

As they walked down the road, it was obvious that it also hadn't been used recently. "Atrus, where is that depression again?"

"Forty meters to your right off of the road. And I still do not detect any movement."

When they finally reached the area, they were horrified to what they saw. It was a mass grave. A pit dug, probably by the same people, then killed, and thrown in. Some looked as if they got in of their own accord. Others were shot with arrows then thrown in. A fire was started on one side but it never took hold and not much was burnt.

James scratched his head. "This makes even less sense than before. If these are the villagers, why would they kill them all, then simply walk away from the village intact? Wouldn't their relatives want their things?"

"Unless there wasn't anyone left that cared."

"You mean the entire families were wiped out?"

Red nodded. "It is very possible. Back in this time it is very common for families to live together and share resources. It makes living far more efficient. Especially when you don't have much. Atrus can you confirm?"

Atrus flashed on in front of them. "Unfortunately I can. Based on the temporal coordinates of 215 BC means this is the work of Qin Shi Huang China's first emperor."

"And that is why these people were killed?"

"I can't say as to what the exact reason is, but Huang's historical account is quite clear. He was a tyrant and killed anyone that defied him. It is possible that these people either didn't approve of something he did. Or helped the wrong person. There were several assassination attempts over the course of his reign. Although all attempts failed, if one of these people were linked to the assassin, it is possible Huang would kill a whole village as an example to everyone else."

Red shuddered. "Another pivotal point in history. Professor Keleeigan sure isn't hitting the low points. I know we got away with no one seeing him in Egypt. But here? There are far more people around, and Huang influenced history for thousands of years. If something changes now, it could have a catastrophic effect on the time-line. And if I remember right he also believed in magic, or at least some really odd stories that had no basis in fact."

Atrus nodded. "You are quite correct. He spent most of his later years trying to find some way to extend his life. He even sent people to find something called the 'elixir of life'. Many of which never returned."

Red snorted. "I think we can assume they didn't find anything and feared returning to the king empty-handed. It would have meant their heads ... literally."

"So what's our next move?"

"Well it is almost dark now. Let's head back to that village. No one has been there for a quite a while and I doubt anyone will be back tonight. We can rest tonight then check out Juyong Pass in the morning."

"Good idea, we both need rest." Red said as they walked back to the small village.

The sun shown brightly as James awoke, sat up and stretched. The mats they found were certainly not as nice as a mattress, but it sure beat the bare ground. "Hello there sleepy head." Red cooed as she nibbled his ear.

"Hello there. What's for breakfast?"

Red grinned. "Whatever you can catch for us?"

Atrus flashed in front of them. "Actually I have a suggestion. There are some fruit trees east of here. Pears if I am not mistaken."

James grinned. "You rarely are Atrus."

"Thank you Sir." Atrus said bowing before his image disappeared.

"Well I will go get breakfast. You make the bed," James said with a wink.

"Okay." Red said as she rolled up the two mats and set them aside. "There, all done."

James turned around in the doorway. "Hmm I think I should have let you get breakfast."

Red grinned. "Too late now. You made your bed, now go sleep in it."

"Actually, I can't, you just rolled it up."

"Har har," she said slapping his behind. "Now get. I will see about making us some tea. There should be some around here."

"Deal." James said as he left and walked down the road and turned down the path heading towards the trees Atrus spoke of. "Atrus? How much farther? It seems to be a larger distance than you originally indicated."

Atrus flashed in front of him. "Sir, I only said it was a short distance away. I didn't give any specific measurement."

"Remind me to redefine your concept of 'short distance' later."

"Yes Sir." Atrus said as he winked out.

After another twenty minutes of walking, he found the trees. Large pear trees loaded with ripe fruit. "Bingo!" But as he reached for one of the lowest hanging fruits Atrus beeped.

"Sir, I detect several people approaching."

"Probably they just want some fruit."

"That is possible; however, do you recall what I mentioned about Zheng? He was a ruthless tyrant that guided every aspect of people's lives. Not knowing the current rules or laws, I suggest we avoid an encounter at this point in time."

"Who?"

"Qin Shi Huang the first Chinese emperor. I neglected to mention his personal name was Ying Zheng, I apologize for my error."

"Don't worry about it. And I think you are overreacting. I am only taking a few pears. Why would anyone care?"

A man appeared in black with white trim wearing some sort of chest armor and a large sword at his waist. "IEO EOLOUACEE!"

"Atrus, I think we have a problem," James whispered.

"I agree."

"Well thank you Mr. Sherlock. I can't even understand him. Do you know what he said?"

"Apparently he said to stop and asked who you are."

"It doesn't help me if I can't respond. Any ideas?"

"Well I could speak to him."

"Oh sure spirits appearing out of thin air and talk to them. Right, that won't have any effect on the time-line," James said rolling his eyes.

"I only suggested it Sir, not that the suggestion was a good one."

"And do you have any practical suggestions?"

"Well I do suggest you refrain from any sudden motions until the A.T.E. can update its matrix."

"Sure easy for you to say. And just how long will that be?"

"Difficult to estimate, some languages are quicker than others."

"Big help you are."

The man was joined by several others. All of them talking to themselves. Then first drew his sword, pointed it at James, and spoke again. "IO AUA AUA? EAECOLE FOU OE!"

"What did he say?"

"He said he couldn't hear you. Who are you? And answer him now."

"I guess I don't have a choice." James said clearing his throat and spoke loudly. "I am getting some fruit. Is that a problem?"

The man looked perplexed. "Eun jod you say?"

James sighed as the translator started working. "I said I am just getting some fruit. Is that a problem?"

"This grove is for the emperor when he travels." The man said placing his sword back in its sheath. "But I suppose one or two won't be missed. How did you end up here?"

"I am new in the area. I decided to take the scenic route as I head home."

The man raised an eyebrow. "I see. Well I suggest you be careful. There are nomadic raiders in the area."

"Really? I am surprised."

"Yes we killed most of them. But one or two got past and ran into these hills. You haven't seen anyone suspicious have you?"

James shook his head. "No I haven't. I will let you know if I do though."

"Good, see that you do. We had best continue on. I hoped to find them here, but there are a few other places for us to search. Come on men." He said as they took off blazing a new trail through the forest.

James sighed as he picked another pear. "Whew that was close."

"Indeed. But there are no raiders in this area. I would have detected them if there were."

"Well they could be outside of your scanning range."

"That is true, but unlikely. The woods only get thicker the farther one progresses from here."

"Well I am not telling them. At least they left us alone. Let's get this fruit back to Red."

A short while later they found Red making tea. She placed some dry wood from a rack near the fireplace and started running her fingers over the wood faster and faster. Until James could no longer see anything but a blur of motion.

After a few moments they caught and burned brightly. She sat back as she heard the scuffing sound of cloth shoes on the hard floor. "Ah good you are back."

James tossed her one of the pears. "Here you go."

"Thanks, but only one?"

"Well let's just say that I'm lucky we got these."

Red cocked her head as she bit into the pear. "Why?"

"When I was about to pick these, solders showed up."

Red's eyes went wide as she swallowed hard. "Solders?"

"Well it seems they were looking for some nomadic raiders that got past them. Thankfully, they let me have a couple of pears."

"Let you? Why would they care?"

"The grove is apparently for the emperor only, when he is traveling in the area."

"I am surprised you didn't shoot them all."

"And take the chance of damaging the time-line? You know me better than that."

Red grinned. "Yes I know you," she said playfully rubbing his backside, "very very well."

James sat down on the floor, pulled a pear from his tunic sleeve, placed it on the traditional Chinese table, and smiled. "Yes you do." He said pulling her over beside him.

By now the small metal pot over the fire was steaming. Red carefully removed it, and poured the tea. She smiled as they ate the pears. "Don't you think it odd that the garrison here would be so worried about one or two raiders?"

"Now that you mention it, that does seem a bit unusual. But we know that Huang was a tyrant and paranoid. Perhaps the men were scared of reporting their failure and losing their lives because of it."

Red nodded. "Yes that is possible. However, wouldn't they make up something at that point? I mean two people escaped, how much damage can they do? Say you got them, and your life is spared."

"Well unless someone else confessed that you lied, then you are dead for sure."

"True," Red said as she sipped her tea.

Atrus flashed in front of them. "There is another possibility. We do know that at some point this year, Huang will go on a tour of the country. Based on the solders comments, and other non-verbal cues, that tour is in progress and this area is next on his list."

Red sat back. "If true, then this is even worse than we thought."

"How so?"

"If Professor Keleeigan's lighthouse shows up here, it could cause their beliefs to change causing a large ripple effect in the time-line. If the emperor is here at the same time that ripple turns into a tidal wave."

James sat back wide-eyed. "Of course. I know we got lucky last time and no one saw Doc. But with so many people in this area, I have doubts it will happen again. Unless ... Doc shows up here rather than in the pass itself."

"Do you think we are that lucky?"

"The way things are going at the moment ... no."

"Any ideas?"

James thought for a moment. "I could try luring everyone from the valley."

"And they would catch you in short order. Not to mention the entire garrison is not going to go running after one man."

James sighed. "True."

"Atrus? Any thoughts?"

"Actually I do. If I use the Shell's projection system in addition to my own, it should be possible to hide the lighthouse for a short period."

"Why would you need to use the Shell's system as well?"

"Because while I can generate large holograms, the proximity to the temporal field requires more power to maintain the illusion properly. I would not be able to maintain it for long if left to my own power reserves. But if I use the Shell's system, since its power system is far larger, I should have enough to maintain the cloak for a short period. Hopefully long enough to get the necessary equipment to Professor Keleeigan."

"Hopefully?" James said, "that doesn't sound very encouraging."

"Well as I said, it will be a large power draw. And considering I have not done this before. I cannot estimate how long it will last."

James stood up and tried not to listen to the creaking of his complaining body. "At least we have a plan. Now we just need to be ready for when Doc shows up. And how in the world do the Chinese stand being on the floor like that all the time."

Red smiled. "I guess you need to get use to it."

"Well I hope we are not here long enough that I do."

Red nodded. "Agreed. And if the temporal coordinates were correct, Keleeigan should show up later today, so you won't have to."

"Good. But one thing bothers me."

"Which is?"

"Neither of us look oriental. In fact, I am surprised the solders earlier didn't shoot first and ask questions later."

Atrus raised his hand with one finger pointing up. "I took

the precaution of altering your appearance with an Asian looking hologram that overlapped your head."

"You gave me an oriental head? Why didn't you tell me?"

"If you recall the solders were too close at the time, they would have heard me."

James nodded and walked over to the doorway looking out to the trees beyond. "You are right of course. But it sounds like we will still need your holographic abilities if we are to keep suspicions about us at bay. How are your reserves?"

"I have almost a full charge. Thankfully giving you Asian features takes far less power than covering you in different clothing."

"At least that is something."

Atrus' hologram disappeared. "Atrus?" Red asked, "Everything okay?"

"Yes. However, I detect people approaching. Likely the same solders James and I encountered before."

James looked up and down the road. "Where? I don't see anyone."

"They just appeared on the very edge of my range. I suggest we depart now, if we wish to avoid them."

"That is strange, I thought you said they were heading in the opposite direction."

"They were."

"Then what made them turn and come this way?" Red looked towards James perplexed.

James' eyes flashed. "Red! The fire you used to make the tea! They must have seen the smoke."

"Dang you are right. I wouldn't have if I knew there were solders around looking for raiders."

"May I suggest we leave now? If we delay any further, we risk the possibility of being seen," Atrus said.

James looked out the door and waved to Red. "Grab the bag and let's go."

Red snorted as she grabbed the bag and walked over to James. "You think I would leave all of our clothes behind? I have been doing this far longer than you, you know."

James put a finger on her lips. "Shhh I know my darling, I know. Now let's go." He grabbed her hand, and they quickly walked around behind one of the houses and started making their way back to Juyong Pass just as one of the solders appeared on the road at the opposite end of the village.

Picking their way through the forest they moved quietly as possible while making sure not to leave any trail behind. After they were halfway up the mountain side James risked talking. "Atrus, any sign of pursuit?"

"Negative, they seemed to have gone off in the other direction, back towards the grove where we were earlier."

"Good, looks like we dodged that bullet," Red said as they continued to make their way up the mountain, less carefully, but still holding James' hand. "Now we need to dodge an even bigger one."

"Anyone ever tell you, you're a real wet blanket sometimes?"

Red smiled and swatted James' backside with her other hand as he continued to lead them up the mountainside. "And you love it."

James grinned. "Well I know you love doing that. Sheesh I don't remember it being this far last time."

"I do, and we were going downhill remember? Uphill is always harder."

"Yeah I know, but it seems longer somehow and these cloth shoes don't help. Can't we put on our normal shoes? They would be hidden under these robes unless we take large steps."

Red shook her head. "Nope. Too much of a risk right now."

"Why? Atrus can hologram us if we need?"

"And did you forget he already has to do our heads, not to mention save enough power to hide the lighthouse when it shows up?"

"Point taken." James said nodding as they finally cleared over the peak. "Whew I never thought we would get to the top."

"Quite the view," Red said looking down into the valley.

James turned and slipped his arm around her waist, squeezed, then looked into her eyes. "I am enjoying this view a lot more."

"Why Mr. Moknkin, did you forget we have a job to do?"

"Never. But it doesn't mean I can't steal a moment here and there."

Atrus beeped. "Or not, I detect an increased level of activity in the valley, especially at the far end."

James sighed. "Atrus leave it to you to ruin the moment. What do you see?"

"I can't quite tell at this distance but there is a large gathering of people there. And it looks to be growing."

"Can you show us?"

"Affirmative. Activating projection." A map appeared showing the valley with a lot of yellow moving dots in the far corner. Several of them seemed to be lining up in a row. "I regret I cannot generate a better image than this."

"And it would take us too long to get down there to see what is going on."

"Wait a sec, could you use the Shell as a spy to give us a close up peek?" James asked.

"Are you crazy? They would see it!"

"Not if Atrus generates a hologram of the sky over it, something like he did to hide you in the wall back in Egypt."

"It is possible," Atrus said.

"But won't that drain its power reserve that we will need for later?"

"If the system is set to recharge shortly after, the effect of it traveling there and back with a small simple hologram projected should be negligible."

Red sighed then handed James the bag she had been carrying. "Okay, do it."

Opening the bag found his backpack and removed the Shell. He then opened the access panel, activated the Shell, and sealed the panel. "Okay Atrus, see what you can do."

"Acknowledged, hover systems have been activated." He said as the Shell hovered up and out of James' hand heading off into the valley. "Activating hologram projection system." Immediately the Shell seemed to disappear.

James smiled. "Perfect."

"Not quite, I can see a little outline between the Shell and the clouds. But it should be good enough."

"Sadly the clouds are changing in an unpredictable fashion and it is difficult to keep up the projection to match," Atrus said.

"Well as Red said, it should be good enough. Just get it down there, take a peek and bring it back."

"Nearing location. Interesting, I am not sure what I am seeing. A lot of the solders are standing on either side of the road. Oh I think I understand."

"Can you show us?" Red asked.

"Yes one moment." Atrus said as a two-dimensional image appeared in the air giving a bird's-eye view of a large number of men on either side of the road. Then several horse drawn carriages came into view, slowly traveling down the center. One of them was even larger and more ornate than the others with its large curved roof and carved inlays.

"That must be Huang, only an emperor would have such a carriage in this time," Red said.

"I concur. Apparently he is visiting today as we speculated earlier." Atrus said as the image flickered and disappeared. "Shall I recall the Shell?"

James nodded. "Yes no need to waste the energy. Now we need to decide what our next move is."

"Do you think the emperor will stay here? Or is he just passing through?"

"If I may suggest, I think he will stay here. At least for the day. I did see a large building that is more ornate than the others. If historical references to his personality are correct, he will prefer to stay in the security of his garrison before continuing on his tour."

"Great, there go our hopes of him just passing through," she said starting to head down the mountain.

"We will think of something," James said stumbling trying to catch up.

They continued heading down the mountain making their way towards the road and buildings.

"Shouldn't we head directly towards the garrison?" James asked.

"And raise their suspicions? Although I doubt they will think anything of two people traveling along the road to see the great emperor."

James nodded. "True, but what is our next step?"

"The best thing we can do is stay in the area and hopefully find Keleeigan before anyone else does."

Red brushed her auburn hair back as a strong wind whipped through the valley. "Atrus? I thought you were bringing the Shell back?" James asked.

"Apologies Sir, I am trying. An air current has developed that is proving difficult to fight against." The wind howled through the valley as it grew in strength. "I may have to land it before damage occurs."

"I didn't think the wind was that strong," Red said.

"It is not, but as it blows through the valley, it is generating unusual sweeping drafts that I am having difficulty anticipating, let alone over coming. I must land before it is damaged," Atrus said as he brought the Shell down as best he could. But even then it did hit a tree or two. "It is down, but unfortunately there were several collisions. However, I do not think the total force was beyond tolerance."

"How much damage occurred?"

"All self-diagnostics say that it is fully functional. I have shut down all nonessential power sources except for the holoemitter to keep it hidden."

"How far is it?" James asked.

"I can do better than that. I can show you." He said as a holo image flashed into being before them displaying the valley and a tiny little blip in the trees right before the road. "The indicator shows where I had to land it, and no one else is in the area. But we will need to retrieve it as soon as possible since the holographic system is still draining the power reserve."

"It will take us some time to get there. Atrus if you are sure no one is in the area why not disable the holographic system for now? If anyone shows up you can still enable it before it can be spotted, correct?"

"Yes, quite correct. System disabled and I will continue monitoring."

The wind continued to whip about. "Good. And is there any change from the other end? The emperor's procession?"

"At the moment I cannot give you details as neither the Shell nor I are close enough. But based on the persons I can still detect, I believe he stopped at the house that was seen before."

"Good," Red said as they continued to make their way through the trees. "Perhaps something has finally went right with this jump."

While they could have made better progress if they first went to the road then walked to the Shell's location, it might have aroused suspicions. Instead, they continued working their way through the rough terrain until they finally found the device nestled up against a tree. James picked it up. "I don't see any damage other than the one dent on the side which I can fix later. I think we got lucky." He said opening the access panel, turning the Shell off, sealing the compartment again, and placing it back in his bag. "There, all safe and sound."

"Good, let's head back to the road. I for one am done with the rough terrain in these shoes," Red said.

"My feet agree with you."

A short time later they reached the wide stone faced road and started walking towards the garrison which they could now see in the distance. "Sir, I detect people approaching."

"Yes I see them," James said, "I hope our holographic faces are on as it's show time."

"Yes, of course, I anticipated your need. And show? What show?"

"Never mind Atrus, and Red better let me do the talking. I suspect they might deal better with a man."

"I agree," Red said giving James a squeeze.

A large group of men approached wearing armor and holding long spears. "Halt! Who are you?"

"We heard of the emperor's visit and wished to pay our respects to the great man who has unified us," James said as he bowed low.

"Is that so? Well we mustn't delay you. The emperor always likes to hear praises from his people. However, please be careful. There are a couple of raiders that managed to get past us earlier and we were sent to reinforce the detachment assigned to find them."

James nodded and bowed. "Thank you. And we will."

The man turned to shout at the men at his back. "Let them pass!" All the men parted on either side of the road leaving a path for Red and James as they continued marching past.

After several minutes the last man was well out of earshot. "Well that was interesting. It seems odd that another detachment would be sent for two lowly raiders."

"It is possible that one or more assassination attempts have occurred by now. Huang was very paranoid after them, probably compounded by his mercury consumption," Atrus stated.

James blinked. "Mercury consumption? Why would he take mercury?"

Red sighed. "If I remember right, back then they thought mercury had mystical powers since it has very unusual properties. Huang also was obsessed with living forever and his doctors probably convinced him that these pills will do that. Or at least extend his life."

"That is correct; however, rather than extend it, it is likely what killed him, and created his odd behavior that was recorded towards the end of his life. If history is accurate, we are at the very beginning stages of his decline."

"I suspect history is accurate. There were several very good historians in this time-line," Red said.

"Then do you think we should actually see him or not?" James asked.

"I would say not, he was borderline insane without mercury. After it, who knows what he might do. One minute be your friend, the next have you killed because of some imagined plot." Red said as she continued to walk down the road squeezing James tightly.

"Not to mention the less contact we have with people at such a pivotal point in history is always good."

Red smiled. "You're learning."

James gave her a squeeze. "How could I not with such a great teacher?"

They soon reached the outskirts of the buildings that made up the garrison and the settlement of people that supported it. By now the sun had dipped lower into the sky as it was late afternoon and scents of cooking filled the air. James' nose twitched. "Mmm get a load of that."

Both their stomachs rumbled. "Yes I know. But I am not sure if we should have further interactions. Perhaps we should leave and eat some of our emergency energy bars."

"I thought you wanted to save them unless we really need them. You know how hard they are to get."

"I know, but I am thinking this is a good time."

"How much damage could be done having one bowl of soup?"

Red smiled. "You are probably right and I am overreacting. Let's eat."

They appeared in the doorway of one of the rammed earth buildings and saw a lady tending a sizable pot simmering over an open fire. "Hello," James said.

The lady whirled around. "Why hello! What brings you here?"

"We were wondering if you might have extra of that wonderful food you are cooking?"

The lady smiled and bowed. "I am Ping. You are most welcome here."

"Thank you," James said bowing lower.

"Please sit, I will get you a bowl."

They both sat on mats in front of a short table as Ping poured a thick porridge into two bowls and passed it to them. Red and James bowed and thanked her again as they took the offered chopsticks and ate slowly. A few minutes later Ping excused herself and left the building.

"If I knew we would be eating boiled millet with chopsticks, I wouldn't have talked you out of eating our energy bars," James whispered.

Red smiled. "Hey it is good for you and chopsticks are not that difficult." She said eating some porridge with a practiced hand.

"Sure easy for you to say." James said as he fumbled with his chopsticks. Hearing a slight beep he looked around but Ping was still nowhere to be found. "Yes Atrus?"

"I think I have detected Professor Keleeigan."

"Where?" Red said as she slipped another bit of mushy millet into her mouth.

"It is difficult to be certain as the temporal signature is very weak. But he should materialize a little south and east of our current position."

"Should? And how long?"

"As I said, I cannot be certain. As for how long that is also questionable. However, I would say within the hour. I believe I can estimate his arrival time better using the previous experiences as an example."

James sighed. "That means you are still guessing."

"Sir, I do not *guess*. I take all the data that is available and draw a logical conclusion based on that data."

James rolled his eyes. "Okay, okay you don't guess, you estimate."

"Thank you Sir, and I think I detect Ping returning."

James quickly ate more of his porridge in what Chinese would consider a rude manner before Ping returned. When she appeared in the doorway, he stood and bowed low. "I thank you Ping for your wonderful hospitality, but we have a long journey ahead of us and we must begin."

"So soon? It is very late, are you sure you do not wish to stay the evening?"

"We thank you but we must be somewhere else before nightfall," James bowed again as Red stood up, "thank you again."

Ping bowed in kind. "I hope you return again to my house."

As soon as they got outside Red whispered. "Atrus? Which way?"

"South and slightly east."

"Which is?"

"Go behind the house and continue in a straight line. I will direct you further as needed," Atrus said.

They looked around and didn't see anyone nearby, then continued on behind the house and walked for twenty meters before Atrus spoke again. "Now turn five degrees and continue for another thirty meters." Atrus said as he continued to guide them. They walked for a several minutes before reaching a location devoid of trees.

"Why aren't there any trees here?"

"I suspect it is due the poor soil at this location. Possibly because of contaminates in the ground that the trees find unsavory. I am detecting a temporal fluctuation. Please step back several meters."

"You got that right," James said as they took several steps back.

Suddenly there was a violent flash of light as a large shape started to materialize in front of them. It started as a large blur then the vague features started to coalesce into the lighthouse. The enveloping temporal field flashed again as the building became fully solid but still encased in the field.

"Get that hologram going now or it is going to be seen! We are not far enough away and this will certainly stand out," Red shouted.

James quickly pulled the Shell from the bag, opened the panel, activated it, then resealed the panel. "Okay, Shell is online. Atrus you know what to do."

"Acknowledged. Shell projection system online. Linking it to my systems, activating it to cover this area." Atrus said as a shimmer appeared behind them. "Hologram activated and is holding. The lighthouse is hidden from view, as are we."

"How long will it last?" Red asked.

"I do not know. The parameters are outside of my level of experience."

"Rough guess then?" James said.

"Rough estimate fifteen minutes."

"Good thank you."

"Give or take fifteen minutes," Atrus said.

"Oh great so in other words you have no idea and it could fail at any time."

"I tried to tell you."

"Never mind." Red said walking over to the doorway. "James! Get over here!"

James ran over in time to see Keleeigan speaking but they still couldn't hear anything. Two people on either side of him looked rather upset. "Doc! How do we help you?"

Inside Keleeigan spoke again. "James! I need you to stabilize the field! We can't take much more of these unstable jumps! Everything in here is starting to fail."

Outside the dark clouds that had been building all day sparked sending a large bolt into a tree nearby. Keleeigan's eyes flashed with an idea and he ran back to his console.

"What are you doing?" Kim asked as he saw Keleeigan's fingers fly across the keys.

"Trying to buy us some time." Keleeigan said as he punched a button opening a panel at the top of the lighthouse and releasing another weather balloon. "I only hope this works."

Outside James shook his head as the dark clouds above flashed again. "What in the world is he doing? He ran back and is typing away at that console. Is there any way he can send a message from it?"

"I am afraid not Sir, no form of normal transmission wavelengths can penetrate the temporal field that is currently enveloping the lighthouse."

"He will find a way."

"Sir, I am detecting a small balloon being launched from the top of the lighthouse."

"A balloon? What the heck for?" James said as he wiped

away some of the rain that was now pouring down his face. Overhead they heard another crack of thunder.

"James! He is trying to catch the lightning."

"Atrus would that be enough?"

"Unlikely enough to pull them out of the temporal field. However, it may succeed in stabilizing it."

Inside Trisia stared at Keleeigan aghast. "Are you insane? How will lightning help us now?"

"Hopefully it will give us enough energy to punch through and keep from jumping again."

"And if it doesn't?"

Keleeigan shrugged. "Hard to say. It could do nothing."

Trisia's eyes narrowed. "Or it could overload everything we have and blow us sky-high?"

"That is theoretically possible, but highly unlikely."

"So YOU say," Trisia snorted.

Outside Red and James were getting thoroughly soaked as the downpour continued. "What can we do?" James asked.

"Nothing that I can detect. Warning! Holographic system is starting to fail. The projection is starting to show gaps."

"Pray." Red said as a large bolt of lightning struck the balloon. But instead of stabilizing the field it flashed brighter and brighter until a whirlpool started in the center of the building causing it to collapse and fold in upon itself as it was sucked in. A second later Keleeigan and his lighthouse were gone.

"Nooo!" James shouted. "It destroyed them."

Red griped James' soaked shoulder. "I am sorry. We did all we could."

"Actually," Atrus piped up, "the power surge did not destroy them."

"What?" What happened then¿'

"It would appear that instead of stabilizing the field, the lightning had the opposite effect. From what I can detect the power did not reach inside where it was needed, instead it intensified the current field causing an immediate and extremely unstable jump."

James brushed the water from his face as the downpour continued. "Do you know where they went?"

"Due to its even more erratic nature, I will need time to calculate the temporal location. Holographic system is nearing critical, I must shut it down now or permanent damage may occur."

"Shut it down Atrus," Red said looking around, "no one in the area anyway."

"Confirmed and shutdown successful. However, I do detect people approaching fast."

"What? Why didn't you detect them before?"

"It would seem that the combination of the temporal flash and hologram hid their approach. May I suggest we retreat to the trees?"

"Good suggestion." James said as the Shell hovered into his hand, slipped it into his pack, grabbed Red's hand, and made a run for it. They reached the other side just in time to see several men emerge.

"What did you drag me out here in the rain for?" One armored man said to another shorter one.

"Sir, I know I saw something odd going on here. It looked like large flashes."

"It was the storm! You drag me out here to get soaked only to see nothing. Wait until we get back to the barracks!"

James sighed. "Well looks like we dodged another bullet."

"Just barely. Let's find some place to stay and get out of this rain."

"Can't we warp out of here?"

"I can't run fast enough in this! It is too slippery, you should know that. Not to mention I'm getting soaked to the skin."

"Right sorry love. Perhaps that house we visited before?" James said slinging the bag over his shoulder.

"We can try." Red said with a shrug.

After some time walking through a torrential downpour, they reached Ping's house and found her sitting by the fireplace. "My goodness! What happened?" she said rising to her feet.

Red smiled and bowed, her long wet hair dripping all over the floor. "We got caught in the storm. We hate to ask, but could we possibly spend the night here?"

"But of course. You can sleep in the side room. I don't have much in it this time of the season."

James bowed. "Thank you. We deeply appreciate this."

"Think nothing of it. I am not about to send anyone back out in this until they have had a chance to dry off."

Red bowed again. "Thank you." They walked past her to the room that Ping had pointed out and closed thin wooden door behind them.

"Well at least we can get dry here," James whispered as he started to pull off his wet tunic.

"Yes, but I don't like imposing on this lady," Red said as the rain pounded the house outside.

"Well we won't be here long, just until the storm passes. And she did offer earlier."

"I know but I have a bad feeling."

"You always have a bad feeling."

"Not always." Red said as she removed the rest of her tunic and hung it up on a peg in the wall.

"Uh-huh," James said as he hung up his.

"Atrus? How long will this storm last?" Red whispered.

"It should be dissipated by morning."

"See? We won't be here long at all." James said as he pulled out the Shell, opened the panel, shut it down, sealed the panel, and hid it back into the bag.

"Uh-huh," Red said.

James stripped off his damp shirt and hung it up next to his tunic. "Did your bodysuit get wet as well?"

Red shook her head. "No, but it dries almost instantly even if it did."

"Funny, all this time and you never mentioned that."

Red smiled. "Well you never asked."

"True." He said sitting down beside her and wrapping an arm around squeezing her tightly. "Guess I should ask more."

"Why Mr. Moknkin, what ever are you saying?" she said batting her eyes.

"You know exactly what I am saying. And after all, we do have some time."

"You know, sometimes you talk too much. Just kiss me you big lug."

Morning arrived with a gentle kiss to Red's cheek awakening her. She sat up with a start and saw James already awake. "Good morning," he said with a large grin.

"Morning. The storm has passed I see."

"Yes sometime in the night," James said chucking a small energy bar over to Red, "I think we had better use these today and get going as soon as possible."

Red caught it in midair and ripped open the wrapping with a well-practiced hand. "Atrus, have you figured out where Keleeigan went?"

"Yes, he went to Siberia 60N, 105E in 210."

A chill ran through James. "Siberia? I certainly hope it is summertime."

"It should be, unless weather patterns were drastically different in that time period. Very little is known about the area at that point in time. However, one good aspect, based on all the information I have, Siberia is sparely populated. We shouldn't have an issue with people seeing us."

"Finally something going right for once."

"No kidding." Red said standing up and stretching. She reached over and felt of the cotton shoes she removed last night, thankfully they were dry and slipped her feet into them. James had his tunic already on and he tossed hers over. She grabbed it in the air and slipped it on.

"Ready?"

Red looped her arm in his. "Always." She said smiling as they opened the door revealing Ping tending another pot of portage.

"Why hello! Did you sleep well? I wondered if I should wake you, but then decided you might need the extra rest."

James bowed low. "Thank you Ping for your wonderful hospitality."

"You are very welcome. As I said, I don't have much use for that room right now, anyway."

Red looked towards the pot cooking on the fire. "You

certainly cook a lot for a lady that does not have any family here."

Ping laughed. "I cook for the solders, it is my job. You can't imagine how much they eat in a day."

Red chuckled. "Oh I *can*."

Ping smiled. "Would you like some? It is hot and fresh. I was about to take it to the garrison."

James bowed. "We thank you for your very kind offer; however, we must be going. We have a long journey head of us."

Ping bowed. "Of course. I wish you a safe trip."

Red bowed in kind. "Thank you Ping."

They both left by the front door and quickly walked down the road for a short distance then before turning into the forest. "Where are we headed?"

"That clearing where lighthouse showed up should be a good place to jump. Nice flat area and no one around," Red said.

"Good idea," James said nodding.

They walked quickly through the forest, eager to jump away from this time-line. When they arrived at the clearing, all was as they left it.

Once in the center, Red removed her tunic and slipped on her normal shoes. "Whew I am so glad to get rid of those shoes. They may have been a great advancement for the time, but my feet certainly don't think so."

James sat down and removed his shoes as well. "You would think that leather would be better. They should know about it by now."

Atrus appeared before them. "Actually Sir, the nobles and above did have leather shoes. It was only the common man that didn't."

"Ah, figures. Something like Egypt all over again."

"History does tend to run in patterns," Atrus said nodding.

"Very true." James said as he tossed his tunic, stood up, then looked over at Red. "Ready?"

"Ready." Red said as she lowered herself into a sprinting position. James got into position and nodded. "Okay let's go!" She shouted bolting in a clockwise direction with tremendous speed. The air began to swirl as she increased her velocity exponentially. In her wake, leaves detached from many of the tress and circled around making it difficult to see.

She pushed a little further and a bolt of lighting struck the center leaving a rip in the very fabric of space and time. Her speed increased again, and the rip opened into a full angry warp with colors fluctuating between red, blue and black.

James didn't like the look of it one bit. "Red, something is wrong."

"I know."

"What is going on?"

"I wish ...I ...knew."

Atrus' image vanished. "Sir, I detect people approaching, they will be in normal visual range in under two minutes."

"Red! Someone is coming! We need to go!"

"No, it is not right!"

"We don't have a choice!"

"Okay, *GO!*" Red shouted as James ran for the warp leapt into it with Red right behind him.

Far off at the edge of the clearing Ping blinked. "Well that is the last time I let guests leave so easily without a proper meal. I am having guilt hallucinations," she muttered quickly heading back to her house.

— 7 —

The air began to swirl kicking up dust into the air. A spark appeared at the center of the wall which quickly grew as other sparks appeared and joined the center intensifying the temporal energy. The energy built until a tear formed and began to grow as though someone was pulling open a zipper. It grew until it was just large enough for a man to pass through.

James crashed out onto the stone floor. He managed to look back before Red fell out on top of him a nanosecond later. The warp quickly sealed itself after.

James reached back and patted her soft backside. "You know we really should stop meeting like this."

"Oh, we should? Why should we Mr. Moknkin?"

"Well, I don't know, people might talk," he said with a wink.

"And who says I care if they do?" she said winking back. "Do you?"

His smile deepened. "Not at all my darling. Not at all."

"Good." She said kissing him then rolled off and started to look around. "Now where are we?"

"And when?"

Red nodded. "And when."

James looked at the various walls with many holes carved into them. There were placed in a staggered geometric pattern. "What is this place?" Peeking out from the end of one of the walls he saw several men wearing togas walking past. Reaching into one of the holes he pulled out a long rolled paper fitted with rods on each end. Writing on the paper appeared to be Greek. He grinned and pointed at the paper in his hand. "Well it looks like Greek to me."

Red rolled her eyes. "Very funny. This must be a library."

"Library? I didn't think there were libraries of this size back when people wore togas like that."

Atrus quietly beeped. "Sir, I believe this is the ancient Library of Alexandria."

James' eyes went wide. "*The* Library of Alexandria?"

"Is there another I do not know of?" Atrus asked.

Red laughed quietly. "I very much doubt that."

James peeked out again from behind the stacks. "Why are we here? I thought we were heading towards Doc?"

"We were. I don't know what shoved us off course. Remember what it felt like in the warp?"

"Yes a bit of a tug and push?"

"Exactly. Something is seriously wrong."

"I have done a detailed analysis of the people in the nearby area and I believe we traveled in distance but stayed in roughly the same time-zone," Atrus said.

"All that and the same time-zone? Ugh. Still, can you imagine what is here? We can actually take a look at the library before it's destroyed."

"This building is another pivotal point in history. Not sure if we should hang around," Red whispered.

"Actually, as long as we maintain a low profile I do not think we would create any changes in the time-line. There were a great many people that used the library. You can be two of those people," Atrus said.

"See? What harm can it do?" James said smiling.

Red peeked around the corner and saw two men talking and walking in the opposite direction. "Okay, if our A.T.E.'s actually get up to speed so we can understand them. That and we are going to need clothes. We don't exactly blend in like this."

"If I may suggest, there is a room on the far side of this building with several togas in a chest, behind a door, in a small storage area," Atrus said.

"And what about their owners?"

"There doesn't appear to be anyone in the immediate vicinity of the togas."

"That will work," James said looking around, "I will go and get them."

"Easier said then done, there are a lot of people around here."

"You forget, Atrus and I have done this before. Atrus, proper clothing please." While Red blinked, James' clothing reformed into a long toga with sandals. "You see? No one will think anything of me other than another scholar."

"You hope. What happens if someone tries to talk with you?"

"I will respond."

"And if the A.T.E. hasn't built an ancient Greek matrix yet?"

"I will give a dumb look and keep ongoing."

"You know, that might actually work," Red chuckled.

James walked down the ornate hall filled with row after row of book stacks. He passed several people talking, but he simply inclined his head and kept on going. "Atrus?" James whispered. "How much further?"

"Keep going in the same direction for approximately another one hundred meters."

"That far? How did you manage to find them so far away?"

"They are on the very edge of my scanners. I only knew they were togas based on the composition and location. Thankfully there is not much cloth in the general area or I would have been unable to locate them."

Passing what looked like the main dining area, then through a garden, James entered the living quarters at the far end. He looked in several unoccupied rooms and finally found the one Atrus had mentioned. Opening the small door on the far wall revealed an ornate chest. Inside he found several togas neatly folded. He grabbed one for Red, one for himself, two sets of sandals, and made his way back to Red.

"Any trouble?"

"Nope, did you expect any?"

"Not really, but one of these days it would be nice not to have to *borrow* clothing."

"Well we couldn't pack for this trip. We never know where Doc will end up next. Not to mention we thought it would be one quick stop in dino land."

"Yes I know. But I still hate it."

"I know." James said slipping on the robe over his shoulders and fastened it at the waist. "And I don't like borrowing clothing anymore than you, after all who knows where it has been."

"At least this stuff isn't as bad as other time-zones," Red said as she slid her feet into the sandals.

"Speak for yourself. I hate sandals and this wool is itchy."

"Well you could just stay in the shadows while I get the lay of the land."

"Ha! If you think I am going to leave you alone, you got another thing coming."

"What do you think? That I am going to meet some beefy Greek guy and run off with him?"

James sputtered. "Well, er no I didn't … I know you … well … wouldn't … "

Red leaned forward and kissed him. "You know you are so cute when you get flustered."

James smiled kissed her back. "Oh hush you. You will get it later."

Red grinned. "Promises promises."

"That my love is a guarantee," he said squeezing her playfully.

"Careful, I might hold you to it."

"My darling, I hope you will."

A voice came from behind them. "Ioloc eioal you?"

They turned to see a large man with a red robe pointing at them.

James just gave a quizzical look hoping the A.T.E. would catch up.

"Who are you?" The man repeated.

James let out a breath he didn't know he was holding, the translator was finally online. "Hello, we are looking at the books here. Are we in your way?"

"No not at all. I just have not seen you here before. You do know it is required to sign out any books that you remove and take back to your quarters?"

Red nodded. "Of course, we will follow procedure."

"Good, see that you do. We lost a very valuable book recently, and I was the one that everyone blamed."

"Sorry to hear that. How could they blame you?"

"Why I am Aristarchus, Head Librarian!"

"Oh our apologies, we did not know," Red said inclining her head.

"That is quite all right, you are obviously new. However, please do follow procedure and be careful. Some books are rather fragile. And a few are even on loan," Aristarchus looked both ways then whispered, "although I doubt Ptolemy will ever return them."

"Thank you Aristarchus, we will take great care."

"Please see that you do." Aristarchus said before removing one of the scrolls from the top of the stack and left.

Red wiped her forehead as she leaned up against one of the stacks.

"What's wrong?"

"Nothing I always get nervous when we encounter important people from history."

"Aristarchus is that influential?"

"Sir, Aristarchus of Samothrace is the head librarian of Alexandria between 181-171 BC and the last one appointed to the position before the great library is burned. He was one of the great grammarian's of the period and the most influential of all scholars of Homeric poetry. Not to mention he was very influential on the design of books from the period and beyond," Atrus stated.

"Okay then a bit bigger than just a librarian."

Red pinged a finger off of James' head. "Yes a bit more than *just* a librarian. And will you keep in mind that this is *the* library? The complex we are in is where we get the name 'museum' from."

"Okay okay, I get the point. But you know that I am always careful."

"Yes but it never hurts to remind you *why* we have to be careful," Red said smiling.

James sighed. "One of these days you will trust me."

Red looked deep into his eyes. "My darling I *do* trust you, I thought I proved that long ago?"

"You did, but then you seem to think I will forget the basic 101's of what we do."

"Sorry love, I guess I keep having flash backs of other people I have encountered. It is not you, I promise."

"It's okay love, forget it. Now what is our next step?"

"Well as you say, shall we check this place out?"

James' eyes sparkled. "Can we?"

Red smiled. "Of course love. I know how much you like libraries."

"Shhhh don't let that get out, or I will never live it down," James said with a grin.

They walked up and down the massive complex. Stacks upon stacks of scrolls dominated the structure. "The history books don't give this place justice," James whispered.

"It is amazing." Red said as she looked at the maze of stacks, scrolls, and columns.

James was looking at one of the upper stacks and didn't notice a man had approached. He bumped into him, sending them both into a tumble onto the floor. Several scrolls fell out of the man's hand and unrolled. "Oh I am so sorry. Please forgive me I didn't see you," James said as he helped the man to his feet.

"It is I who should apologize. You are clearly new here, and I should know better."

"No it was truly my fault." James said rolling up the scrolls and handing them back.

"Nay it was mine. And I Demosthenes apologize."

Red gave James a simple tap, and he saw her stern look. He

bowed towards the man. "Of course Demosthenes, I humbly accept."

"Thank you. Now that our concentration is already broken, would you join me in the dining area?"

Red smiled. "Oh no we couldn't think of intruding on your meal."

"It is no intrusion at all. I am staff here after all and I am obligated to help our scholars in any way possible. I think you will enjoy the tagenias especially, the cook has an amazing talent for them."

"Thank you. I am sure we will." James said as they followed him to the main dining area. "Atrus? What is he talking about? The A.T.E. didn't translate it."

"The tagenias or tagenites is a type of pancake that the Greeks made for breakfast."

"I am surprised they don't have more Egyptian cuisine."

"Well this is the largest port in the world, and Greek is the universal language at this point in time. Not to mention some of the greatest scholars of the period were Greek," Atrus whispered.

They walked into a large courtyard encircled with more columns and many rectangular tables in the area. Several men were seated eating and Demosthenes sat at an empty table motioning to join him. "Please."

James nodded at and sat looking up to Red. Demosthenes smiled. "Your lady is welcome to eat with us. While our custom is to have the men eat first, we can and will make an exception."

"Thank you," Red said sitting down.

Demosthenes motioned towards the servants. "Please serve us. What would you like?"

"Well you did mention something earlier?"

"Oh yes of course. Tagenias for them and myself."

The servant girl nodded. "Of course."

A few minutes later she returned with plates of pancakes and fruit.

"That was fast." James said looking at the large plates full of food.

"Well we usually eat at this time of day and since this is the most requested item, the cook usually has several being made." Demosthenes said as he took a piece dipped it into a kind of sauce on the side and popped it into his mouth.

James noticed the lack of utensils and did the same. It was good, although the sauce was not as sweet as he expected. He popped another piece into his mouth as Demosthenes finished his. "I am sorry but I must get back to work. Please stay and enjoy. I have instructed the servers to bring anything you like."

"We thank you," Red said smiling.

"Think nothing of it." Demosthenes said as he left the room.

"Well that was odd." James said after the man was well out of earshot.

"Actually it isn't," Atrus whispered, "he was apologizing, and you weren't accepting. In many cases that can escalate into a heated confrontation in this time-zone. As if he was too low in status to apologize to you."

"Oh my, I certainly didn't want to give that impression."

"I know and notice I didn't kick you this time," Red said.

James smiled as he ate the last of his pancake. "I noticed and thank you. Now can we go back to poking around for a bit? Or do we need to find a place for you to rest?"

Red shook her head. "Nope I'm fine. We can look around."

James smiled as he stood. "Oh good."

They walked back over to the center of the library and

James began to poke around the books. At one point he pulled Atrus out so that he could get a more intensive scan of the books in a stack without anyone seeing the green beam. When he rejoined Red, his grin was wide enough to swallow the sun. "This is amazing. They have so many originals here. *The Iliad* and *The Odyssey* and apparently in homers own hand! Can you imagine it? A true first edition!"

Red nodded. "Yes they even steal any books that happen to be aboard ship when they come into port, make copies and give the owners the copies. I also found out that the books Aristarchus mentioned, Ptolemy paid over one thousand pounds of precious metal as a guarantee of their safe return. But many here doubt that he will ever return them just as Aristarchus said."

"Do you think that is going to cause problems?"

"I doubt it. At least nothing was ever recorded. It is more likely that Ath?nai won't go up against Alexandria because of the power it now holds over the world. Knowledge is power and now Alexandria has that power."

"It is still amazing." James said as he went back to the stacks.

They spent the rest of the day looking through the library's vast collections, with Atrus translating much of what they were seeing. Up and down the great stacks, many people were examining the scrolls. Several staff members were also returning books to the stacks and making notes in the index. One could see this is where all modern libraries were founded.

"Oh hello," a man said to James almost bumping into him, "do you have any specific interests?"

"Not really, I just love knowledge."

"Ahh a man after my own heart. I am Periandros. I

also do not have a specialty, but rather enjoy all knowledge. Although the study of mathematics is of particular interest."

James smiled. "Then you are in the right area. Some of these scrolls contain wonderful knowledge in mathematics."

Periandros bowed slightly. "Thank you, I will partake of this knowledge." He said pulling one of the scrolls off of the stack behind James and left.

Red leaned over and whispered in James' ear. "What was that all about?"

James shrugged. "I have no idea. I can't imagine why he was asking me all of that."

"Sir, I detected deviations in his voice pattern. He is very nervous about something."

"Nervous? I wonder why."

Red sighed. "Hey, we are here to poke around then leave. Not get involved in politics."

"Who is getting involved in politics? I just wonder what he was nervous about. I have this feeling he has something up his sleeve. Er toga."

"And what are you going to do about it? Follow him around? You are going to get us both thrown out!"

James grinned. "No I won't." He said sneaking off into another row. After a few minutes he found Periandros looking at several scrolls on history, then he moved on to another section filled with maps. Red tapped him on the shoulder which caused James to spin around fast. "Geeze! Don't sneak up on me like that!"

Red smiled. "Me? I didn't do anything."

"Don't give me that innocent act, you don't do it very well."

"Uh-huh." Red said as she lowered herself behind James. "So what is he up to?"

"Nothing much, just looking at books. If he was nervous, he sure doesn't seem to be now."

"On the contrary, his heart rate is still elevated. I can detect it even from this distance," Atrus said.

"He probably feels like he is being watched. Which he is. Come on let's head back to the living quarters. Demosthenes offered us his room for the night."

James turned. "He did? When did you two get all chummy?"

Red laughed then kissed him on the cheek. "You know you are cute when you are jealous."

"I am not."

"You are," Red said as she kissed him again.

"I have a bad feeling about this guy."

"And I say you are blowing smoke. Just leave him alone."

James gripped the stack. "Do you trust me?"

"What? Are we going to go through this again? Of course I trust you!"

"Then listen to me. All my training says this guy is going to do something. I don't know what, I don't know when, but something."

Red rolled her eyes. "Okay okay, we will watch him for a bit longer. But if nothing happens we go and rest then warp out of here. Deal?"

"Deal." James followed the man as he continued to wind his way throughout the library. But suddenly he headed towards the private area in the back. "Ah-ha! I knew it."

"What is back there?"

"I don't know, but it is for staff only."

"How do you know?"

James pointed to the sign above the doorway. "The sign says."

Red looked up to a large carved sign that straddled two columns, clearly stating in several languages the area was for library employees only. "So it does."

They followed him and found the room full of blank scrolls, tables, and ink wells. Along with raw papyrus being made into scrolls. "Looks like the book making factory behind the library."

Red looked over James' shoulder. "What in the world is he doing?" In the corner Periandros stood there playing with something in his hands moving it faster and faster.

"I can't quite tell, it is a little dark in here."

"Sir if you like I can elevate the light level in this room."

"No Atrus, we don't want to scare everyone in the library."

"Actually no one would see it except us, but as you wish," Atrus replied.

"What is he doing?"

"I still can't tell, but did I see a spark?" James said squinting.

"I thought I did too. A very faint one."

"Atrus can you tell what he is holding?"

"Not at this distance without attempting an intensive scan."

"Dang it."

"I just saw another spark."

"So did I. Is he trying to light a pipe?" James asked.

Red shook her head. "There aren't any pipes in this time-zone at least not the kind you are thinking of."

"Oh no!" James shouted as he ran forward.

"James! You can't–" Red started to say, but he was already gone.

"Periandros! Stop!" James shouted as he watched something small burn brightly in Periandros' hand.

The man gasped as he looked up. "I must! In the name of Caesar this place must burn!"

"No!" James shouted, but it was too late. Periandros threw the small lit object into a pile of dried papyrus. It went up a second later spreading to the desks and the blank scrolls in the room. In a few moments the whole room was alive with the sight, sound, and smell of fire.

Red caught up with James and grabbed his shoulder. "We have to get out of here!"

"But the library!"

"It is too late, we have to get out of here!"

"No!" James shouted and ran from the room into the main area. "Fire in staff room! Grab all you can and get out of here! Save the books!" Men jumped out of every corner grabbing scrolls off of the stacks. Some had bags, others filled their arms with all they could carry.

"What do you think you are doing?"

"Trying to save some history before it burns!" James said as he grabbed several scrolls. Above, the flames had spread to the main roof structure, and it was only a matter of time before the whole building burned.

Red sighed and grabbed a few scrolls following James outside. They found Aristarchus guiding people to a small brick building off to the side. "Put all the books in there!" They watched as men ran back inside grabbing more books trying to save them from oblivion.

James turned around to see the whole library in flames. A tear ran down his cheek. All that knowledge gone. And all because of one fool. James felt a hand on his shoulder and he turned to see Aristarchus smiling. "I hear you were the one that first told us of the fire. For that I thank you. If it wasn't for you, all would have been lost."

"But the building, all the–"

Aristarchus shook his head. "The building we can replace. The knowledge we cannot. But thanks to you, we saved most of it. We will rebuild. Have no fear. The Great Library of Alexandria will rise again. And if there is anything that I can do for you, you only need name it."

"Well we could use a room for the night."

Aristarchus smiled. "Take my room in the residence section."

"But the fire?"

"The only thing that burned is the Library building itself. The rest is separated for this reason. So please take my room, it is the largest one and I would be happy if you used it. It is because of you, we didn't lose everything. It is the first one on the right."

James bowed slightly. "Thank you, we are honored." He reached for Red's hand and nodded towards the other end of the complex.

Red stood by smiling then took his hand. They calmly walked towards the rooms and found Aristarchus' first one on the right just as he said. They closed the large ornate door after them and locked it. "So why aren't you reaming me out?"

Red smiled as she sat down on one of the chairs with elegantly carved legs. "*Me?* What ever do you mean?"

"You know exactly what I mean. I was fully expecting you to tell me how not to get involved in the time-line."

Red smiled. "I don't know what you are talking about."

"Uh-huh. What do you know that you are not telling me?"

Atrus flashed in front of them. "I believe that Red is not alarmed as the Great Library of Alexandria had several fires.

There was only one that was total and complete, before that not much was lost."

"You mean that I did the right thing?"

"Let's say you didn't do anything that history didn't already record. At least what survived over the centuries. You saved a few books, which was very noble. While they do get destroyed in a few years, they get a reprieve for now."

"Why didn't you tell me that it was futile and I was crazy?"

"Well you looked so adamant and who knows, perhaps you saved a book that spurred on Erasistratus, Euclid, or even Hipparchus. You did save several books on mathematics after all."

James sighed as he sat down on the simple bed with its linen sheets. "Well at least we got a decent room out of the deal."

"Love, if you recall, I already got us one. Demosthenes offered his as well."

"Yeah and he was just looking to get into your pants when I wasn't around. Er tunic."

Red laughed. "You are so cute when you are jealous."

"I am not."

"You so are." Red said smiling as she walked over and sat down beside him.

"Well we should get some sleep." James said as he lay back and pulled Red down with him.

"Hey! Who said I want to sleep with you?" she said grinning.

"Oh I don't know. Perhaps me." He leaned over to kiss her soft lips.

"Well well, presumptuous aren't we Mr. Moknkin?"

"Where you are concerned, you bet I am."

"Mmmm so you say."

"Atrus?"

"Yes Sir?"

"Hold all our calls."

"I don't understand, there are not any phones in this time-zone."

"Never mind Atrus, never mind."

The sun gently streamed in between the curtains gently waking James. He sat up fast to find Red already up sitting on the chair next to the bed. "Why didn't you wake me?"

"You appeared to need it."

"You are the one that needed rest more than I. You drive, I just ride along."

"Oh you do more than that my darling," Red grinned.

"Well you certainly do take me around the world." James smiled as he rubbed her hand.

Red leaned forward and kissed him. "My darling that is so mutual."

"Well I guess we have stirred up enough trouble here. Shall we see if we can reach Doc this time?"

Atrus flashed in front of them. "Stirred up enough trouble? I do not believe you created any trouble, only helped."

"Another one of our old expressions Atrus. Meaning we have done enough here and should move on."

"If that is what you intended, why not just say so?" Atrus said as his image vanished.

Red shook her head. "Sometimes he sounds so much like a computer."

"I heard that!" Atrus said.

Red smiled. "I know you did."

James stood up and stretched, then grabbed his bag and slung it over his shoulder. "I do wish we could have looked at the books a bit more. I mean how many people actually get to read the *Iliad* and the *Odyssey* in Homer's hand?"

"Actually, quite a few Sir," Atrus said.

"I meant after the library burned down."

"Oh, I see your point."

"You do?"

"Yes you wished to further explore the works that were later lost to the world due to fire or passage of time. You needn't worry though."

"Why?"

"Because I scanned most of the work and can reproduce it in holographic form at any point."

"Atrus! You scanned it *all*?"

"Well not all, but I did manage to scan a vast majority of it covertly."

James danced around the room then sat back down on the bed. "It is not the same thing as holding the papyrus in your hands, but after we save Doc, I am definitely looking forward to reading those."

Red leaned over to nibble his neck. "And here I thought you would want to spend time with me instead of a bunch of dusty old books."

James looked at her directly in the eyes. "My darling you can never compare to a dusty old book."

"Good."

"The book would always win."

"Hey!" she said swatting him.

James laughed. "Only joking my love, only joking."

They opened the door, and not seeing anyone, slipped out and off the Musaeum grounds. They headed south out of the city and after a while found a lone flat area. James reached down to feel the earth under his feet. "It feels hard enough. This will work don't you think?"

Red felt the grass and pushed her hand into the dirt. "It is a little softer than I like, but I have jumped in worse. I'm ready when you are."

"My darling you do the hard part, I just tag long," he said slipping her another kiss, "you call it."

"Okay let's do this!" She said lowering herself into a sprinter position and bolted off running in a clockwise direction. The air began to swirl faster and faster. Dirt and dust kicked up into the air and followed Red in her wake.

Atrus beeped. "Sir, I detect people approaching at a rapid pace."

"Already? Red hurry!"

"I know! I know!" She said pushing her speed a little further and lightning shot down opening a crack in the very fabric of space in time. The crack glowed an angry red then blue, then fluctuated between black and red as it slowly grew in size. "It is harder than before. I don't understand it."

"Reeeed, we are going to have company any second."

"I know! Almost there." She pushed a little faster and the warp ripped open just big enough for a man to enter. "Go! Now!"

The person in question is very close. They will be in visual range in ten seconds."

"I can't take the risk. Red go without me!" James said going off to see who was nearby.

"WHAT?" Red shouted but James was already off running. "James! Get back here and jump! I can't keep this open!"

James ran fast and when he came to the rise jumped to his belly and crawled over the edge and peeked over. There was a man running towards them. James took out the gun, set it for stun and carefully aimed from the cover of the thick brush on either side of him. "Atrus let me know when I will get him and when he won't see it coming."

"Acknowledged. Two degrees to your right, three up, hold, down one. Wait a moment. It is a lock." James pressed the trigger and a near invisible beam lanced out and caught the man in the chest as he looked in the other direction. He stopped mid-stride and went down in a heap. "Good shooting Sir."

"Now let's get out of here." James said as he ran back to Red's position. The warp had shrunk a bit, but she hadn't left. "Red I am here."

"Then jump! I am over spent!"

James ran for the warp, Red gave one last burst enlarging it slightly. He jumped in with Red right behind him.

Inside they felt the same odd tugging and pushing sensation as before. Then almost as if they ran head-on into something, rubber-banded back. Finally after what seemed like days–but was only a few minutes–a tiny rip appeared and engulfed them.

Lightning struck as the air swirled around. A bird squealed as it tried to fight the strong wind. A crack formed, then the rip slowly opened wider and wider. The red-black warp seemed angry as James crashed out landing on the stone street. A second later Red landed on top of him. The warp slammed shut as though it had never been.

"Ugh, I love you, but you need to lose some weight."

"Hmm? What did you say? Okay love."

"I was kidding my darling. Are you okay?"

"Am okay, just tired. Why did you leave?" She tried to punch him in the arm but it wasn't even a slap.

"Someone was coming, I couldn't risk them seeing us leave. You are the one always telling me not to leave loose ends."

"Hmm? Okay, whatever you say."
"You rest my darling, I will find us a place."

8

James stood up and looked around. Buildings on either side of the street stopped in a dead end at the one side and intersected another street on the other. "Another alley, just great. But at least no one saw us land," James muttered.

The stone streets didn't look modern and the solid building design looked Greek in nature with the corner accents. "Atrus? What kind of buildings are these? They look concrete."

Atrus appeared before him. "Hold me out that I might do an intensive scan." James nodded and held Atrus' cylinder out as a green beam grew out from the tip and connected to the wall going up and down then retracting. "They are concrete in fact."

"But Greek's didn't have concrete."

"No, but Roman's did. The architecture is similar to Greek. They did after all adopt any Greek methods and designs as their own."

"Rome? Well, at least for once we might have a leg up on the clothing department."

"I do not understand Sir."

James reached into his pack and pulled out their tunics and sandals from Alexandria. "For once I kept these when we jumped." He said slipping into the tunic and robe then started to dress Red. "I'm glad this is easy to put on her." He said as he carefully pulled the long dress tunic over her head, affixed the robe then tied the belt in place. "She is going to get quite a shock when she wakes," James said with a smirk. "Ah well, when in Rome ..."

"I am not sure I follow that statement. Of course we are in Rome."

"Never mind Atrus, never mind."

He slung the linen bag containing both of their backpacks over his shoulder, carefully pulled Red to her feet, wrapped her arm around his neck, lifted her into his arms, and moved to the end of the street. The scene before him took his breath away. There, just beyond, was the Circus Maximus stadium in all its white gleaming glory.

The streets were crowded with people, carts, and a few animals. A man approached and pointed. "Teia oac xpeialeote bonoeia?" James gave a blank look continued on.

Atrus beeped quietly. "Sir, he was asking if you needed help."

"I had a feeling, but I couldn't respond in English, now could I?"

"I will endeavor to speed up the translation matrix."

"Since when?"

"Since the last update you did, I created a short range sub link that allows for me to access them remotely."

"Oh, handy."

"It should be. Please stand by. There are a lot of people talking in the area, it should be enough to update the matrix."

James moved slowly across the road holding Red. "Well I can't move fast that is for darn sure."

Another man approached.

"Teia oac. I aem is the kupia injured?"

"Excuse me?"

"I said is the lady injured? I am a doctor. My name is Gellius."

"She just collapsed, I think it is the heat and will be fine in a few minutes."

Gellius nodded. "Ah of course. If you like I have a place she can rest, it is across the street."

"Thank you, but I don't want to leave her."

"Leave her?" Gellius asked looking perplexed. "Oh, you may stay as well."

"I wouldn't want to intrude."

"Now what kind of Roman doctor would I be if I didn't offer my humble office in a lady's time of need? Please I insist."

James nodded. "Well if it isn't an intrusion. Then of course I accept."

"Would you like help with her? I can call my servants."

"That is not necessary, I can manage. Please lead on."

"Of course." Gellius said as he walked across the street to a large building. James followed as fast as he could carrying Red. Inside the building wasn't just one man's room, but a honeycomb of rooms. Apparently this was an earlier form of the modern office building or apartment complex. Gellius led them down several tile covered hallways and stopping at one on the far end. Drawing out a key he opened the lock and ushered them inside. As soon as they entered, two female servants stopped what they were doing and approached Gellius. Both were lithe and in their early twenties. "They will cater to your needs." Gellius said as his hand waved openly towards them.

Both women bowed slightly. "Of course Master."

Gellius turned to leave. "Stay as long as you need."

James raised an eyebrow. "You are leaving?"

"Yes I have an appointment in the government section of the forum. I am sorry I must leave now or I will be late."

James nodded. "I understand perfectly. I thank you for your assistance."

"Think nothing of it." Gellius said with a wave of his hand as he slipped out and closed the door after him.

The tall blonde women in a very short white toga stepped forward. "How may we serve you?"

"All she needs is rest. Do you have a couch or somewhere that she might lay down?"

The shorter woman adjusted her knee length toga then flicked her long black hair back as she tilted her head from side to side. "A kline? We have a kline in our Master's room." She said leading James over to a side area closed with long draping fabric. Inside they found a couch with expertly carved legs covered with a long intricate well padded pillow. One side was higher than the other giving the whole thing an inclined feel. James carefully placed Red's head on the higher end and her feet towards the lower. Smiling he kissed her forehead.

"She means a great deal to you," the first woman said.

"Yes she does."

"How may we be of further service?"

"Do you have any water? And perhaps a small piece of cloth?"

"Of course. We do not have any fresh, but we will fetch some from the local well."

"Oh no need if you don't have any available. She will be fine."

"Our Master told us to take care of you. And we will.

Besides, we needed to go to the well anyway. Please wait for us."

James nodded. "Of course and thank you."

James watched as the women opened the door, placed two large poles into the handles of a large pot, lifted it up and left through the door. "I didn't want that much water," James muttered to himself.

"Sir, I believe they are required to keep a fresh supply of water here and she indicated they needed to go anyway. It is likely their supply is either exhausted, or tainted in some fashion prompting them to resupply," Atrus said after the door closed.

"I am sure you are right, but still it feels as if I gave them an order."

"Sir, you didn't. They asked how could they help, you asked for water, and they are complying."

"Still it sure felt like it. Ordering slaves, I never thought I would be in this situation."

"Sir, if the concern you are feeling is because they are forced into something they do not want, their voice patterns when they spoke with Gellius indicate quite to the contrary."

"Oh?"

"Yes, the patterns indicate a great amount of admiration and thankfulness when they spoke to Gellius."

"They? So you are saying that both women wish to be slaves?"

"I cannot say what their wishes are, only that they seem to be pleased, or showing gratitude in their current situation." A moment later Atrus' image turned towards the door then back again. "They are returning." Then he flickered and disappeared.

A moment later the ladies opened the door hauling their

large clay vessel of water. They carefully sat it down, removed the poles that were in the handles, sat them in the corner, and closed the door. The first woman drew some water from the large pot using a small cup, poured it into a glazed bowl, then handed it to James. He tentatively took the small bowl. "Thank you."

She noticed his reluctance. "Is everything all right?"

"Yes, well no. I mean I don't feel right giving you commands."

The woman cocked an eyebrow and shrugged her shoulders. "Why? We are servants."

"Well it feels awkward for some reason."

"There should be no reason you should feel awkward." She stopped and looked back to make sure the door was shut tight. "Wait are you escaped slaves?"

"Oh no, not at all."

"Then I do not understand your reluctance. Don't you have your own servants?"

"Can I ask you a question?"

"Of course."

"How did you come to lead the life you live?"

"You mean how did I become a servant?"

"Yes, if you don't mind me asking."

"Not at all. I am proud of my work. I was orphaned at a young age, and I did not have the resources to take care of myself at the time. I had several options and becoming a servant to a good man was my best choice. I am very thankful for Gellius, he treats us well and not as slaves. We have been invited to accompany him several times when he speaks in the forum. It is a great honor. Soon we will have our citizenship, but even then I think I will stay with him. He has given us so much."

The second woman nodded. "Yes, my story is similar. Gellius is one of the nicest men I know."

"Well he certainly was nice enough to us. Oh do you have a piece of cloth I can use? A small one will do."

The first woman opened a cabinet and removed a small ragged piece of linen and handed it to James. "Will this do?"

"Yes that is perfect, thank you." James said dipping it into the cool water and placing it up on Red's forehead.

"Are you sure she is all right? I can go get Gellius."

"She is fine, or will be. It is just simple exhaustion."

"If you are certain." The first woman said while bowing and backing away.

James sat for a couple of hours, never leaving Red's side. Finally her eyes fluttered open. "Ugh get the name of that Mack Truck."

James took her hand. "I'm right here love."

Red tried to sit up then thought better of it as the room began to spin. "Okay, perhaps sitting up is not such a good idea. Where are we?"

"At a doctor's office."

Red looked down at the toga she was wearing. "Funny I thought I left this behind."

"You did, I grabbed it right before we jumped. I had a feeling it might come in handy."

"Where are we?"

"Shhhh don't worry about it, there is plenty of time for that later."

Red squeezed his hand her eyes stern. "Where are we?"

"Rome apparently."

"Rome! Roughly the same time?"

James nodded. "Looks like it. I haven't been able to confirm yet."

Red rolled her eyes and fought not to have her head follow suit. "You only need to ask someone the date. Remember they should have the Julian calendar judging by this room."

"Well, taking care of you was more important than finding out the date."

"You don't understand. Something is seriously wrong. I have never jumped three times and been unable to reach further in time than this. We should be centuries ahead, not in almost the same time-zone as before. Did you see anything when we were traveling?"

James shook his head. "No, but on more than one occasion I felt as though we ran into something or hit something. Or were pushed forward then rubber-banded back. It was a very odd sensation."

Red sighed. "I had the same feeling which doesn't make sense. Atrus? Do you have any data on the last couple of jumps?"

Atrus flashed on in front of them. "Of course."

James glared at Atrus then cleared his throat. "Atrus? Your hologram?"

Atrus smiled. "If you are referring to the two young ladies that helped you earlier, they have left the area some time ago."

"They did? That is odd I didn't hear them leave."

"You were busy tending to Red at the time. I did not see a problem with them leaving so I did not bring it to your attention. Was I in error?"

"No, not at all. I just found it odd I didn't hear them. Okay what data do you have on the previous jumps?"

Atrus projected a two-dimensional image of various graphs displaying energy and matter along various data lines. "As you can see as we tried to push forward, energy was absorbed then reflected that gave the sensation of being pushed back. The other time when we were pushed in the opposite direction it was as if something ran us over. The mass energy was very high at that point, I cannot explain it."

Red's eyes flashed. "Atrus, can you super impose the data of the pushing field in a three-dimensional nature?"

"Hmm possibly. One moment." Atrus closed his eyes, and another image took form next to the first. This was in full 3D and took more and more shape as the data was applied. Eventually it looked like a tall featureless building.

James' mouth dropped. "The professor's lighthouse!" He said before the image was complete.

Atrus filled in the rest of the data quickly and did a compare. "You seem to be correct, the data does take that image."

"But how? He is waiting for us to go to him, we know his temporal location."

Red nodded. "We do yes; however, you forget that time is not a straight line. We could be feeling the moments he was in the warp trying to move from one time-zone to another. Hence we are colliding with him since our signatures are somewhat similar, but then his is so much larger, it runs us over."

"Does that mean we will always have this problem?"

"No I suspect it is because he bopped around in the warp several times before actually landing. We are encountering his temporal wake, if you will. And since he is so much larger, it is causing–"

"Us to wipe out?"

"Exactly. Which also begs the question, he shouldn't be having this kind of effect unless he is destabilizing the whole warp somehow."

Atrus raised his hand. "If I may suggest, it may be due to his high-powered field that is extremely unstable now."

Red snapped her fingers. "Of course! The instability of the field compounded with the massive size compared to us is giving the warp one heck of a seizure." Red said trying to sit up but lain back down when the room spun again.

"Then how do we fix it?"

"We find the professor as soon as possible. The next jump we should be able to reach him. I hope."

"Are you ready for another jump?"

Red shook her head. "Not quite, but almost. Just a little more rest. And this sure beats the caves we have been in."

"No kidding. Although Aristarchus' room was nice as well."

"True, but I bet Demosthenes' was nicer," Red grinned.

James rolled his eyes. "You and that guy again."

Red leaned forward despite herself and kissed his lips. "You know you are so cute when you are jealous. And I love you for it."

"So you say. So what did that big, strong, hairy, Greek guy have on me anyway?"

Red laughed. "Not a thing my darling."

Red stood up and held on to the couch for support. "Are you sure you are up to this? I mean you can rest more, and you look to need it," James said.

"No I think we had better go. I don't like staying here for any longer than we need. This doctor sounds fine, but I think we had best be on our way."

"Well won't you need to rest before we jump again?"

"I will, I just won't move fast. I can build up my energy if I walk slowly and don't exert myself. And moving around is better considering we don't want to attract attention."

James sighed. "Yes, you are right of course."

Atrus' hologram faded. "The two servant women are returning."

The door opened and the two ladies from before appeared. "Hello, we thought you might like some fruit? Oh you are standing! Are you feeling better?"

Red smiled. "Yes I am feeling much better thank you. And we thank you for your help."

The first woman smiled. "It is Gellius that you should thank."

"We will, where is he? Still at the forum?" James asked.

The second woman nodded. "Yes he should be there."

James nodded. "We will thank him personally and mention how helpful you were."

"That is not necessary, we did very little. And after all it is our duty to obey Gellius."

"Of course, but we wish to mention it to him, nonetheless." James said standing and took Red's hand. "Thank you again."

Both women nodded and opened the door, then closed it after them. Immediately Red wrapped her left arm around James' neck. "Okay so perhaps this wasn't one of my better ideas."

"Are you all right?"

"Yeah, the world keeps trying to spin a bit. Just don't let go."

James laughed quietly. "My darling when have I ever let you go?"

Red smiled. "Never to my knowledge."

"Yes and I never will. So keep that in mind."

"My darling, I never could forget it."

"Good," James said smiling.

They walked outside of the building complex and down several streets when James stopped to look around.

"What's wrong?" Red asked.

"I am not sure. I thought I saw someone following us."

Red looked around. "I don't see anyone."

"Yes I know. Atrus? Is anyone following us?"

"It is hard to ascertain given the great number of people in the area and the short time we have been here. After a longer period I should be able to tell with more certainty," Atrus whispered.

"Great. Can you at least tell us where the Forum is?"

"Yes. Down this street, take a left, then down that street and take a right. It should be at the end."

"Wow, I didn't know you had accurate maps of ancient Rome."

"I don't, but it is the greatest concentration of people, and given how central the Forum was to every aspect of life during this time-zone, it was a logical deduction."

"Okay thanks Mr. Spock."

"Mr. Spock? My name is Atrus."

"Atrus it was a joke. Never mind, I will explain it some other time."

"Acknowledged."

They moved with slow careful steps down the street while watching the great number of people. Some stopped to look at them for a minute, most gave them a quick glance and moved on. Or ignored them completely.

When they almost reached the Forum, Atrus beeped. "Sir, I now believe you are correct: we are being followed."

"I knew it. Who is it?"

"That I cannot ascertain. The person is using the great number of people here to their advantage, I can't get visual lock. However, I do know they are following us based on the movement, and when we stop so do they. It is too coincidental."

"Agreed. Are you sure you can't get more information?"

"Not without doing an intensive scan and having everyone in the area seeing my scanning beam."

Red sighed. "No we can't have that."

"Affirmative. One other suggestion would be to use the Shell, I could use its holographic abilities as before to keep it hidden while searching for the person in question."

"It is too risky to get out with so many people around at the moment. And if we go somewhere else, we may tip off our shadow."

"True. Then I am open to suggestions as to an acceptable course of action."

"Atrus? Is there another dead end alleyway we could use between us and the Forum?"

"Yes there is one ahead of us on the left. But considering that disappearing was not in your best interest before. I do not see how that helps."

"Never mind. I have an idea." James said as they slowed their pace. At the last moment they slipped into the alleyway and he set Red up against the building for support and moved to the very edge of the structure. He pressed himself against the brick and waited.

After a few minutes he heard something and his instincts took over. He leaped from the alley, reached out grabbed an arm, spun it around and pressed the persons face into the brick. It was all over in a microsecond. The blonde woman from Gellius' office stood her eyes wide, paralyzed in fear.

"Why are you following us?"

"Gellius said we were to take care of you. If I said you

left, he may not have been pleased and would ask where you went."

"But I had told you I was going to meet him at the forum."

"Yes you did, but I had to be certain. If you didn't or were distracted, I needed to have an answer for my Master. Can you release me please? You are hurting my arm."

James let go of her arm and stood back. "Sorry. I knew someone was following me and I needed to find out who."

"Why?"

"I thought perhaps it was someone out to rob us."

The woman nodded. "That is something to fear I am sure. But not in the middle of Rome with so many people watching."

James smiled. "You are probably right. You can go back, we are going to the Forum as we said."

The woman rubbed her wrist. "Yes I see. I am sorry I did not mean to alarm you."

James smiled and raised his hand. "Think nothing of it. You were trying to anticipate your Master's wishes."

The woman bowed slightly. "Yes of course. And do you have to mention this little incident to him?"

"Of course not. Just go on back. As far as we are concerned, it never happened."

Red pushed off of the brick building she had been leaning against as the world finally stopped spinning. "Yes nothing happened."

The woman smiled and bowed low. "Thank you." She said before heading back towards Gellius' office.

The crowds grew more dense as they continued down the well-worn street. Even such an exceptional example of Roman construction could not hide the millions of feet trodding upon it.

Smells of fresh baked bread, among other wonderful smells wafted through the air as merchants tried to sell their wares. The Forum was not only the center of government, but of commerce. It was the very lifeblood of the city, and the world around it. The early morning sun had already heated the pavement to the point they could feel the warmth through their sandals.

"What exactly are we going to do when we find Gellius?" Red whispered as one of the merchants tried to get them to buy some of his baked goods.

"I don't know. I guess thank him, we told the girls back there we would. But I wanted to see what he was up to. Something is not quite right with the man."

"What do you mean? Because he helped us?"

"Yes he did; however, what doctor do you know of that wouldn't postpone an appointment if a patient needed it? Instead, he was in a hurry to leave."

"You are right, I didn't think of that. Although I didn't talk with him."

"I doubt you would have picked up on it. I have a feeling, that there is more to this doctor than meets the eye. I can't imagine why a doctor would want to go to the Forum so badly when they have a patient in their office."

"Didn't you tell him that I would be fine?"

"Yes, but that is not the point. Doctors usually try all they can and won't leave a patient like that. And he has to run off to the Forum?"

"Couldn't it be he had another patient he was meeting?"

"At the Forum? Not likely, that would be done in his office. Unless he is doing something political."

"Political? What could a doctor of this time do that was political?"

"I don't know, it was just an odd thought. Have you ever been to Rome before?"

Red shook her head. "Not for any length of time. I passed through once, but didn't meet anyone. And I think it was a different time-zone judging by the buildings. They look much newer than when I saw them."

"Hmm. Atrus?" James whispered as he looked around.

"Yes Sir?" Atrus whispered back.

"Did you scan Gellius when he was in front of us?"

"No, an intensive scan would have been visible and expose me to those in this time-zone. You have always instructed me to take the utmost care in avoiding that."

"Yes I know. But did you get any information about him at all?"

"Well I did a weak passive scan if that is what you mean. His heart rate was elevated, and he was sweating. However, I deduced it was from the clothing and the climate."

James nodded. "Could be, or it could be something else."

Red snorted. "Well I know I am sweating under this toga, so why wouldn't he?"

"Technically, you are wearing a stola. Although the under layer might still be called a toga," Atrus whispered.

"Picky picky." Red said rolling her eyes.

James looked around again. "Would it hurt to check him

out? After all, you always wanted to find out about any doctor that was examining you before."

"Yes. However, you said he didn't examine me, not to mention the other times were in the far future. Here, they don't have the technology to be the same kind of threat as the future doctors."

"True. But don't you find him the least bit suspicious?"

Red sighed and shrugged her shoulders as she put her arm through his and resumed walking. "I suppose we can check him out, if it will make you feel better."

James grinned. "It will love."

"Okay now the next big question is ... where is he?"

"I have no idea. But he must be around here somewhere."

The crowds had become much more congested the closer they got to the Forum. Atrus waited until there was a large enough break in the crowd before he risked speaking. "Sir, I have located Gellius, he is near the furthest end of this area."

"Where Atrus? There are a lot of people here." James said as he looked up and down at the large number of people that only seemed to increase.

"To be more specific, the temple on the far left I detect someone matching his general body shape and clothing."

James squinted in the intense sunlight. In the distance he spotted a man talking with another to the right of a pedestal platform. A third man walked up to the platform and shouted for attention.

While looking at this new speaker a man walked up and stood in front of James. "Good day citizen, can I interest you in some freshly baked bread?" He said offering up a loaf. The scent of the bread wafted to James' nostrils and his stomach complained loudly. He couldn't even remember the last time they ate, regardless it felt like years from now. A smile crept across his face as he realized it was years from now.

"No thank you." James said forcing his stomach to be silent. It was too risky buying bread from this man, not to mention he didn't have any money.

"Are you sure? Perhaps your lovely lady would like some?"

"No, I am fine. Thank you," Red said smiling.

"Perhaps some wine then?" The man said taking another step closer and producing a flexible container with a long neck from the bag he carried.

"No thank you. We are fine, and if you will excuse us," James said.

"Are you sure? It is a very hot day." The man said taking another step closer to Red.

James' senses went on alert and he spotted a hand reaching for Red's bag peeking out from the side of her tunic. He lashed out and grabbed the hand just as it touched the exposed flap. "What do you think you are doing?"

The man suddenly grew anxious. "Citizen, you misunderstand, I am trying to be helpful."

"Helpful to my lady's property you mean!"

"Citizen! I am an honest man!"

"Hardly! Now be gone before I take my revenge!" James said as his eyes narrowed.

The man bowed low. "Of course citizen, I humbly obey."

When he was out of earshot Red turned to James. "How did you know there wasn't any real police in Rome?"

James grinned. "Did you think I slept through all my history courses? I remember one professor saying that he was amazed there wasn't total chaos due to the lack of a real police force during this time."

"I still think Atrus told you."

"Actually, to my own amazement, I did not," Atrus whispered.

"Hey now! No fair, two against one," James said chuckling.

Red poked him in the ribs. "For once he is on my side," she said grinning.

James looked around but could no longer see the man in the location Atrus mentioned. "Atrus? I don't see him."

"I have lost my lock as well. I suspect he went into one of the buildings near the Rosta."

"Rosta?"

"The podium up there where that man just gave his speech." Red said gesturing towards the rectangular shaped stone platform at the very edge of their vision.

"Hmm perhaps he was here to meet someone," James said scanning the large crowd.

"I told you. Now let's find a place where we can warp out of here."

James raised his right hand with one finger pointing in an upward angle. "Not yet, I still want to see what he is up to."

Red rolled her eyes. "*Still?* He is just doing his day-to-today business."

"Perhaps, call it a hunch," James said as they continued on. Near the Rosta, people packed the Forum either waiting for a new speaker, looking at the rules posted on the nearby columns, or conducting their own private business. Slowly they made their way through the crowd to the Rosta, but Gellius was still nowhere to be found.

"Now were?" James said looking at the entrance of several large buildings.

Red shrugged her shoulders. "This is your hunt. You pick."

James gestured towards a large columned building to their right. "That looks as good as any."

Red nodded. "Okay."

They passed several statue adorned columns in the open to reach a larger structure at the other side of the Forum. As the surrounding crowd thinned, Atrus beeped.

"Sir, I believe I have found Gellius," Atrus whispered.

"Well don't keep us in suspense, where is he?"

"Behind you, in the Basilica Julia."

James grunted. "Well why didn't you tell us *that* before."

"Because I lost him in the crowd, which I mentioned previously."

"Atrus, I didn't want an answer."

"Then why did you ask the question?"

James rolled his eyes and sighed. "Never mind."

They turned around and made their way back through the crowds to a much larger structure on the other side of the Forum. Inside they found a labyrinth of rooms. Each room contained everything from bankers doing their trade, to civil courts in session. Even merchants selling their wares to officials and spectators alike. On the far side they saw areas etched into the marble floor with several games similar to chess in progress.

Finding a corner some distance from the crowds James whispered. "Okay where is he?"

"Towards the middle, he is talking with one of the merchants."

Red scanned the crowd and spotted a man some distance from them looking around in quick movements. "You are right, he does seem to be nervous about something. And what is he buying from that merchant?"

"It is difficult to tell from this distance, but I suspect it is Atropa belladonna," Atrus whispered.

James cocked an eyebrow. "Deadly Nightshade? What the heck would he be buying *that* for?"

"There are many uses for the plant, and he is a doctor. It is possible he is acquiring it as an ingredient for a medicine?"

"If that was the case, then he wouldn't be acting this way. He would be confident, not looking over his shoulder."

"I have to agree. No way he has done this before." Red said looking away before Gellius could notice her gaze. "Okay we found him, now what?"

"We go say 'hi'." James said as a grin slowly crossed his face.

Red's eyebrows connected as she frowned. "Don't you think that is going a bit far? May I remind you this is all history and we might change the time-line?"

"I have a hunch."

Red rolled her eyes. "Oh well if you have a hunch …"

"Hey you have trusted my instincts before."

"Yes, but they are not always right either, you know."

"Okay, okay, I give you that. But can it really hurt just to walk up to him and say 'hi'? After all, we did tell the servant girl that we were going to talk with him."

Red sighed as she looked over to Gellius who examined another piece of nightshade, smiled, nodded, and placed several coins in the merchant's hand. "Okay, you got me there. It looks like we have to, or it may cause problems for the servant."

"Right," James said taking Red's hand, "let's go greet the good doctor."

They walked quickly over to Gellius who had turned to

leave the Basilica Julia. "Gellius?" James said raising his hand.

The man froze and slowly turned around. Sweat glistened on his forehead and he looked relieved when his eyes focused on James. "Oh! It is you! I see your lady is doing much better."

"Yes, she is. I hope you don't mind but we wanted to thank you in person for your assistance."

Gellius continued to sweat but smiled despite himself. "Think nothing of it. I am a doctor after all, it is my duty to help those that are sick or injured." He said with a wave of his hand, then walked closer lowering his voice. "How did you find me?"

"You told me you were going to the Forum, remember?" James said smiling.

Gellius looked to the sky, grabbed his slightly protruding stomach with his free hand, and laughed. "So I did, so I did."

"If I may ask, what is that plant you are holding?" James said pointing to the bit of green clutched in the Gellius' hand.

Gellius started sweating even more than before. "This? Oh, I use it in several of my medicines."

"Which ones?" Red asked.

"Several actually."

"Are you all right? You seem to be sweating a lot and it is not that warm," James asked.

"I . . . I am fine, thank you for your concern."

"You are quite welcome. And if I may ask what medicine are you making today? It must be very difficult to use nightshade as an ingredient."

"You . . . *know* . . . what this is?"

James nodded. "Yes, of course, it has many uses but can be deadly if not handled properly."

Gellius nodded and released a long-held breath. "Yes, very true. However, being a doctor I do know how to use it. In fact, I am making a medication today for Caesar to treat his head pains." Gellius looked around and lowered his voice a little further. "He has had several lately and is in a great deal of discomfort."

James nodded again. "Of course, let us not delay you further. And we thank you again for your assistance earlier."

Gellius inclined his head slightly. "You are most welcome as I said. Now if you will excuse me I need to head back to my office and prepare this."

"Of course," James said.

"Oh and your servant girls tended to us well. One would only stay at your office when we mentioned coming here to see you," Red said smiling.

Gellius turned back to face them. "Thank you for letting me know. They do serve me well." He said turning away and left the building.

Red gave James a gentle kick. "Ow! What was that for?"

"You forgot all about the servant didn't you? The whole reason we came here in the first place?"

"Er ... well ... I ... that is ... "

"Oh hush you," Red said kissing him.

As they left the Basilica Julia and the nearby crowds Atrus beeped softly. "Sir, I believe I have seen some further unusual behavior with regard to Gellius."

James looked around. "Which is? I don't see him."

"He left the immediate area, paused for a short period, appeared to throw something between two structures, then continued in the direction of his office."

"That is odd, and I am sure you want to check it out," Red said with a sigh.

"Yes love, if you wouldn't mind."

"Well we have come this far, I don't see why not?"

"Atrus, where exactly?"

"Southeast of our position. Walk straight, past the two buildings, then turn right," Atrus whispered.

They walked down the streets feeling the increasing heat of the road through their sandals. In a small space between the buildings they found the plant Gellius was carrying. Red picked it up and looked at James. "Why would he throw this away? He just bought it, and it had to be expensive."

James' eyes flashed. "Could it be he was planning on poisoning Caesar?"

"Not possible, he was stabbed not poisoned," Red said dropping the nightshade to the ground.

"Unless he was planning on it, and we just changed history to what should have been. Atrus? Did you determine the date?"

"Yes based on the various news postings on the columns in the forum and a few overheard conversations, I have determined today is March 13th 44 BC."

Red cocked her head as her eyes went wide. "March 13th 44 BC? Are you sure?"

"Yes. Based upon all the data available, that date is accurate," Atrus stated.

James turned towards Red as they both stopped. "Does that mean what I think it means?"

Red nodded. "Yes, it is two days before Caesar's assassination."

"You are quite correct," Atrus said.

Red's eyebrows met as she chewed her bottom lip in concentration. "This doesn't make sense."

"What doesn't?" James said.

"Gellius was purchasing nightshade right?"

"Yes? So? He said he was using it to make something for Caesar ..." His words trailed off as he looked even more perplexed then his eyes went wide. "Wait a minute! Are you saying I am right and he was planning on killing Caesar himself?"

Red nodded. "Exactly, and would explain why he threw it away. He had second thoughts after talking with us."

"Then we actually had a part in making history turn out as it should? And you didn't want to go to the forum." James rubbed Red's elbow with his own.

"Don't remind me. But now I am worried."

"Why?"

"Because if we altered the time-line perhaps something else has changed."

"I have run several simulations and I doubt that to be true. However, I will admit that humans are very unpredictable so my simulations will never be 100% accurate."

"Also if I may suggest we continue our pace. There are several people looking in our direction. It would appear that we are attracting unwanted attention standing here immobile."

"Quite right Atrus." James said as they resumed their leisurely walk down the well-worn street then leaned towards Red's ear. "Do you really think something has changed in the time-line?"

"I don't know. But we can't risk it. We have to make sure that nothing has been contaminated by our actions. This is a pivotal point in history, it could have ripples that could build into a tsunami of changes."

"Then what do you suggest?"

"We need to stay here and make sure history unfolds as it

should. Find Gellius again and make sure he does not change his mind a third time."

"Okay I agree, but how do we find him again?" James said as they passed several temples and the various merchants called out to sell their wares in front of them. "Rome is a big city. And while we could wait for him at his office that would really set off his suspicions."

"If I may suggest, at this time of day with business concluded, it was common for people to visit the baths. They were a large social center. Even if we do not locate Gellius, someone else might know his location," Atrus whispered.

"Hmm, well I guess when in Rome," James said with a slight shrug.

Red smiled. "You do realize that you will have to strip down, place everything you own in a little box they provide and hope no one steals it, right?"

"You have a point there, and that is something we cannot risk."

"Well if you wish to give that appearance, there is another option. I can project the proper image and eliminate the need to leave anything behind."

"That will certainly work. As long as I don't sit down."

"You can sit down without concern. Or you can wear a subligars," Atrus stated.

"What is a subligars?"

"A simple loin covering garment, the equivalent to a swimsuit."

"A swimsuit? Wouldn't we stick out like a sore thumb?"

"Actually, the first recorded use of the bikini was during the Roman empire. Therefore, if you use the underclothing or subligars for the bottom and Red wears the strophium or top that you acquired with the togas, it should give a very commonplace appearance."

"Well I am glad I kept everything then." James said as he padded his linen bag concealed under the toga, wrapped an arm around Red, and squeezed. "So do you want to go swimming with me?" he said with a wink.

Red rolled her eyes. "I don't know about this, but Atrus is right. It is the best way to find Gellius."

"Atrus? Where is the bathhouse?"

"Thermae they were called, and there should be one located three blocks away on the left."

Red raised an eyebrow. "Your maps include a listing of all the bathhouses?"

"Not exactly. While I do have a general map of the city, as I mentioned before, not all structures are labeled. But in this case I can determine the location by the rising steam some distance from us."

James looked up to see the large steam clouds oozing from a building several blocks away. "Guess I should have just looked up."

"Well, if it is any consolation, I thought it was smoke," Red said with a grin.

"The fourth cloud on the buildings far right actually is smoke from the burning of fuel to heat the water in the thermae. Therefore, technically, you were correct."

"Atrus, you are not helping," James said as his eyebrows met.

"But I was ... oh ... " Atrus said as his whisper trailed off.

9

They managed to get through the crowded streets this time without incident. While the heat of the day grew more oppressive, it still had not dampened the activity. If anything, there were more people than before. Standing before the towering concrete structure, James pointed to the large sign by the door. "Atrus, what does that say?"

"It says that admission is free to all citizens today and reminds us to thank Magistrate Nigellus. Often political figures would pay for such facilities to sway a vote or to gain popularity."

"Well, some things never change it would seem," James sighed.

"It works out for us though. As I didn't bring any Roman money did you?"

James quickly felt around his tunic. "Er no I didn't. I didn't think of that." Walking inside, the grand entry gave way to a large enclosed courtyard with various activities going on. Everything from weight lifting to several games being played with people running around passing large balls. Everyone wore minimal clothing consisting of a loincloth and the ladies had an additional band of fabric around their breasts.

A man approached them. "Welcome! Today's services have

been paid for by Magistrate Nigellus. Be sure to thank him, he is currently in the tepidarium," the man said pointing to a room to their right, "you can change in the apodyterium or the tepidarium if you prefer. And the lady may use all the facilities today."

"Thank you, and she will," James said with a slight nod.

"The pleasure is mine, I live but to serve." The man said as he bowed low and backed away.

"Well? Where to?" James said wrapping his arm around Red and giving a gentle squeeze.

"Let's try the tepidarium, after all Magistrate Nigellus is there, and wouldn't Gellius want to visit the man paying for the day?"

"Good idea," James said nodding. However, when they entered the large ornate mosaic encrusted room they stopped in surprise. "Atrus! No one is wearing swimwear here!" James grunted under his breath.

"Well it was debated by many historians if they actually used them in the bath houses or only when exercising."

"*Now* you tell us!"

"I can still give you the proper appearance if you desire."

"Not right now with everyone looking!" James said out of the corner of his mouth as he gazed around the room. Off to the side he spotted the entrance to an adjacent room with several merchants selling food, and people eating their purchases while sitting on ornate benches staggered around detailed tables. "We could wait in there," James whispered nudging Red in the direction of the restaurant.

Looking in, she noticed the people were wearing clothing varying from nothing, to the loincloth of the subligar, and even a few with full togas. "Yes, we should fit in without having to change."

The restaurant area, while less decorative than the tepidarium, was no less impressive. The tables were topped with marble containing inlaid metals in several patterns encircled with matching benches. James sat at a vacant table with Red sliding in across from him. A man quickly approached wearing a subligar with a short, thin cloak over his torso. He smiled and leaned forward as he spoke. "Welcome citizens, what can I get you today? We have bread, fish, fruits including apples, pears, and of course, wine on hand. Not to mention some more specialty items, which I can tell you and the lady prefer, including dormice in honey or even snails. I can get something else though if that does not appease your tastes. You have but to ask."

"Nothing thank you," James said.

The man frowned. "Nothing? Then why did you come in here?"

"We are meeting someone," Red said.

"Yes, perhaps you know him, Gellius?"

"Gellius? The doctor? Yes he comes in here almost daily. I hope you are not sick."

"No, of course not," James said shaking his head, "we were talking earlier and then remembered something else after our business was concluded."

"I see. Well he should be in soon. Please feel free to stay here as long as you need. And if you get hungry waiting, call me." The man said as he turned around to attend to three dripping men that just entered the room.

The table, being located by the doorway, gave them a clear view of the tepidarium and the rooms beyond. James sat back a bit to shift his gaze around the large men that appeared in the doorway. "I hope Gellius shows up soon," Red said leaning forward. "I don't like this."

"Don't like what? We are just watching for Gellius, he will show soon. As Atrus said, the baths were a Roman's favorite pastime. And for a doctor, I would think even more so."

"I know. But there are too many people here, and at a pivotal point in history. It makes me nervous."

James looked into Red's eyes. "I know, I am not happy about it either. But what choice do we have?"

"I know, I know, but I still don't like it."

"Well neither do I. If you want, we could order something to pass the time. Oh I know, how about a few dormice smothered in honey? He did say they have that on hand."

Red's face scrunched up as her tongue shot out. "Yuck! How could you even suggest that!"

James leaned forward and kissed Red's scowl. "You know I love it when you make that face."

Red's eyes softened as a smile crept across her lips. "Oh hush you."

Over an hour later many people had come and gone, but still no sign of Gellius. James shifted his position on the hard marble seat. "These seats may look impressive, but in comfort they truly fail."

"Well you were the one that wanted to wait in here." Red said rolling her weight to her other loudly complaining hip. "I think dirt floors are more comfortable."

"No argument from me on that. And I think we may need to leave, anyway."

Red looked around. "Do you see Gellius?"

"No. But what I do see is not good."

"What do you mean?"

"I have noticed that several people have been watching us. That kind of attention we do not want."

"Where?"

"Two in the tepidarium, and two others at the table on the other side of the room."

Red turned her head slowly then back again to not draw attention. "Yes I see them. What do you think? Thieves?"

"Could be. Or curious as we have not ordered any food yet have been sitting here for some time. Hard to say. Either way I think we had better move on before their curiosity gets the better of them."

Atrus beeped softly. "Sir? I believe I have located Gellius."

Red shifted her gaze back and forth. "Where? I don't see him."

"It is difficult from your position. To your left, the far corner, near the recessed area for changing."

"I still don't …ah." Red said as her eyes located Gellius placing his items in one of the hutches carved into the wall for clothes. A woman with long blonde hair stood next to him, inclined her head then began to help him remove his toga.

"Looks like one of his slaves has joined him at the baths." James said as the woman finished removing Gellius' toga and carefully folded it.

"And the one that was following us earlier," Red said as she stood up.

"Yes that is her," James said standing, "well let's go see the good doctor."

It took several minutes to leave the restaurant and cross the tepidarium. By the time they reached Gellius, he had removed all of his clothes except for one small piece of fabric that hung down from his stout middle. Seeing them approach, his eyebrows met and sweat pooled on his forehead, but he quickly brushed that aside with a large grin. "Hello again! It is good to see you so soon. I have never seen you here before, I assume you are enjoying the free facilities today?"

James nodded. "Of course, who wouldn't?"

A balding man wearing only a subligar and waving a branch over his shoulder so that the leaves impacted his back as he approached. His smile could swallow a whale. "Gellius! So glad you could make it today. And who are your friends?"

Gellius inclined his head. "Magistrate Nigellus, how could I not come today thank you for your gift."

Nigellus waved his hand dismissively. "Why Gellius you are always welcome you know that. Of everyone here today, I am glad you could attend most of all."

"You honor me Magistrate Nigellus."

"What is with all the formality? Call me Nigellus. I may have payed for the bath today, but that does not mean you need to kiss my feet. Just remember this when I am up for reelection." Nigellus leaned forward lowering his voice to a notch above a whisper. "Which incidentally is next week."

Gellius' eyes widened as he leaned back in feigned surprise. "Oh is it? I had no idea."

Nigellus' smile broadened. "No, of course you didn't. And who are your friends?"

Gellius' feet shifted uncomfortably on the mosaic encrusted floor. "Well, we just met a little while ago, this is our first trip to Rome. He was nice enough to help us earlier today," James said.

Relief washed over Gellius like a great flood. "Yes the lady was not feeling well, and I took them to my office."

"Sounds like our Gellius here, always trying to help people. I am sure it is why you became a doctor in the first place. I am Nigellus, as you are no doubt now aware, and please remember me at the election."

"Someone that would pay for today on such a large scale? We could never forget your generosity. Thank you Magistrate Nigellus."

"Please call me Nigellus today, thank you. I am very glad to see your lady is feeling better, and you were able to bring her."

"Yes I am feeling much better, thank you Nigellus," Red said smiling.

"Wonderful, and I assume you have a place to stay tonight?"

"No, we had not found a location yet. But we did pass several inns that should suffice." James said holding his right hand on his toga to make sure it did not move out of place.

"A inn? That would not be wise for citizens such as yourselves. If you didn't know, most of them are run by pleabean's and not worth your time. I would also be wary of one's possessions in such an establishment. Gellius has a large domus, I am sure he wouldn't mind letting you stay the night. It would be much safer for voting citizens such as yourselves I can assure you. Right Gellius?"

"Of course Magistrate Nigellus. They are most welcome to stay with me for the night."

"How many times do I need to tell you, today it is just Nigellus. Well I have many other voters, er citizens to greet, if you will excuse me." Nigellus said as he walked towards another group of people who had entered the tepidarium then turned to speak over his shoulder. "Please enjoy yourselves."

"Thank you for putting in a good word for me with the magistrate, now can you tell me why you are here? Who sent you?"

Red shook her head. "No one sent us."

"I do not believe you. Someone must have. You can tell them I will not do as they asked. And in fact you helped me see that."

"Tell who?" James said blankly.

Gellius looked into his eyes, cocked one eyebrow, and his stare softened. "I am a good judge of character and I am sorry I implied otherwise. You are welcome to stay at my domus tonight. It may not be what you are used to, but certainly better than any inn. Not to mention safer."

"We wouldn't want to impose–" James started to say.

"Nonsense! I have plenty of room."

"If you are certain it is not a problem," Red said.

"I am," he lowered his voice to a barely audible whisper, "And if you don't accept I will never hear the end of it from the magistrate."

"Well in that case, we would not want you to get into trouble with the magistrate."

"Thank you. Now I would show you to my domus, but I need a bath badly." Gellius said as he started heading towards the pool at the center of the tepidarium.

"Or you could tell us and we can go there," James said.

Gellius stopped and turned around. "Even if I told you that I live five blocks north and three east you wouldn't get past Jovinus."

"Jovinus?"

"He is my ostiarius, among other abilities. He used to be in the army, but wanted to leave after the last campaign. I have known him for years and gave him a job. After all the years of carrying heavy armor into battles, watching my domus is easy work."

"I see, perhaps you could send your girl here to tell him we will be staying tonight?"

Gellius shook his head. "He would not believe Thaleia. I have told him to only accept my word on such matters. Besides, I need her here. And didn't you say you were here to avail yourselves of the thermae? Why do you want to leave so soon?"

Red nodded. "You are right, we cannot leave without enjoying the magistrates wonderful gift."

"Good. I will have Thaleia find you before I leave. Enjoy." Gellius said as he walked over to the water pool in the center of the room and carefully slipped into its warm embrace.

Thaleia moved closer and bowed slightly. "Why are you here?"

"What do you mean?" James said cocking his head.

"Are you here to threaten me?"

"Not at all, why would you say that?"

"If you are here to tell Gellius what happened in the alleyway, then do so. I will not have it held over me. There is no reason to delay, I will not disobey my Master."

Red leaned closer. "We are not going to tell Gellius. We made a promise, and we'll keep it. What happened then will always remain between us."

"Then why are you here?"

"We are here to enjoy the thermae that Magistrate Nigellus has graciously paid for today."

"And that is all?"

"Yes."

"Then I owe you an apology."

James waved his hand dismissively. "Think nothing of it."

"Thaleia? I need you," Gellius said waving from the pool, "bring the oil and the strigil."

"If you will excuse me, my Master requires me." Thaleia

said bowing then picked up a bottle, a long metal rod with a flat area at one end, and walked over to the pool.

"What is that used for?" James said raising an eyebrow.

Atrus beeped softly. "The strigil is used to scrape the skin after oiling. Soap in this time is a very high end luxury and not commonplace."

"Well, shall we take a dip?"

"I can watch everything if you want to," Red said.

"I would advise against it. I did a very passive scan of the water in the pools and by my estimates, it has not been changed in over a month. That compounded with all the people using it for cleaning, and the lack of soap, the bacteria cultures are running very high," Atrus said.

Red and James shuddered in unison. "I think I'm done with the whole Roman Bath experience. How about you?"

"Agreed. But now what do we do? I think Gellius is going to be a while," Red said.

"You could check out the library, it is the room to the right of the restaurant. It is not quite as warm and no one would think anything of someone sitting in there for a prolonged period," Atrus stated.

"They even have a library here?" Red asked.

"Well I am sure it won't rate compared to Alexandria but it will meet our needs," James said with a wink.

After a few minutes they found a location between two of the three stacks that gave a clear view of the tepidarium pool and Gellius soaking in it. After twenty minutes two men approached Gellius and sat down on either side of him in the pool.

"Hmm this is not normal judging by Gellius' face." James said indicating with his elbow, making sure that anyone looking at them would still assume he was enraptured in the scroll held between his hands.

"Yes he looks as white as a sheet, even more than when we met him in the Forum." Red said gazing up from her scroll then lowering her eyes back down a second later.

"Too bad we can't hear what they are saying."

Atrus beeped. "I can tell you what they are saying."

"How? Did you get an upgrade you didn't tell me about? Last I knew that was well beyond your range."

"Actually while it is beyond my normal audio pickup range at the current levels; however, because he is in a clear line of sight I can tell you what they are saying by reading their lips."

"Well don't just tell us about it," Red said.

"Acknowledged."

Gellius looked back and forth quickly between each man. "Thaleia would you go get another bottle of oil?"

"Master, the bottle here is over half full."

"And I want a new bottle, that special kind I like. Please fetch one."

"Yes, Master." Thaleia said as she bowed, placed the towels, oil, and strigil near Gellius and left the tepidarium.

After she was well out of earshot Gellius turned towards the man on his right. "What do you want?"

"You know what we want. You agreed with the plan. Everything was all set, now we hear you have not upheld your end of the agreement."

"I have changed my mind."

"You can't change your mind now!" The other man said as his eyes narrowed.

"Yes I can and I do. I will not have any part of this or any future plans. A citizen has shown me today that what we were planning is wrong. There are other ways. If you want to continue, you can do it without me."

The man on his right shook his head. "Gellius ...Gellius ...Gellius you don't get it. You don't have an option. The wheels have been put into motion, there is no stopping it now. This is far bigger than you."

"That may be true, but I will not have his blood on my hands."

"You will regret this."

"You don't have anything on me. My conscience is clear. To expose me, would expose yourselves just as much. And you won't risk that, so don't waste breath with threats you cannot enforce."

The man on his left leaned closer. "We never make threats, we make promises." The man growled before both of them got out of the pool and left the tepidarium.

"I am sorry that I cannot repeat what they said after leaving the tepidarium, I could no longer passively scan their lips at that distance," Atrus said.

"That is okay, I think we can guess the rest."

"And I think our good doctor has had enough of the bath for today." Red said nodding in Gellius' direction who by now had left the pool and began replacing his toga and sandals. "I think we had better join him before he leaves us behind."

"No kidding." James said as he replaced the scroll he was reading just in time to see Gellius leave the tepidarium.

"He is leaving in a big hurry, let's go!" Red said grabbing James' hand. They left the library through the tepidarium, crossed the palaestra with several games still going on and were outside a moment later.

"Where did he go?" James said looking up and down the street. "Atrus? Do you have a lock on him?"

"Negative. However, based on the directions he gave us earlier, I believe I have located his domus. I assume that is where he went."

"Agreed. Which way?"

"Down this street for several blocks. I will guide you as we go. I would generate a map, but this is too populated of an area," Atrus whispered.

"Yes Atrus, very wise." James said as they walked. The sun was setting by now and while the crowds had thinned a bit, it was still easy to bump into someone if you weren't watching.

By the time they reached Gellius' domus the sun had long past set, and the streets were getting quite bare. Only a few people left heading home, even the merchants were too busy closing their shops to try to sell them anything.

The domus was large. Iron bars covered every window. A sizable man, wearing armor that only left the area below his knees exposed, stood at the front door. "Are you Jovinus?"

The man's eyes narrowed as he looked at Red then back to James "Yes. Who are you?"

"We are friends of Gellius and are staying with him tonight." James said as he placed his arm around Red and squeezed.

His eyes narrowed further as his hand gripped his sword, readying to draw it instantly should he need. "He did not tell me. I am sorry but you will have to leave."

"He probably forgot to mention it, he has a lot on his mind."

Jovinus drew his sword part way out of its sheath. "He

always does. I am sorry but I am under strict orders. You must leave now or I will remove you by force."

Thaleia approached from behind and placed her hand upon Jovinus' shoulder and squeezed slightly. "It is okay, I was there when Gellius invited them for the night."

Jovinus didn't move other than to turn his head towards her. "Thaleia you know the rules, I cannot admit them without specific orders."

"Will you at least let them stay here while I get him?"

"I suppose I can wait a few minutes. He always gave me discretion on how or when I use force."

"I will return shortly." Thaleia said as she turned on her heal and disappeared inside.

"I noticed the bars on the windows. Do you really have that much problem in this area?"

Jovinus' body did not move except for his lips. "Being a noble, you should know. Unless you have stolen the toga you are wearing. If you are attempting to distract me, you will find it won't work."

A hand reached up from behind Jovinus and rested on his shoulder. "Jovinus, it is true, they are staying here tonight," Gellius said.

Only at the word of Gellius did his stance soften, and his sword slide all the way back to its scabbard. "Yes Sir. I am sorry, I did not know they were your guests."

"Nor did you have any way to have known. Think nothing of it. For tonight you are to give them every courtesy. No one else is to be admitted. Understood?"

"Certainly. No one will get past me tonight."

"Of that I have no doubt. Please come in and enjoy everything I have to offer." Gellius said while motioning for Red and James to enter.

"Thank you," Red said, "you are most kind."

Gellius ushered them past the entrance into a large room with a decent sized pool in the middle. At each corner were expertly carved statues that matched the marble walls of the pool. Above the pool, the roof was open with a hole the exact size of the pool itself. Along the matching marble walls various paintings hung, which James guessed were only slightly less expensive than the statues. Along the walls, and in various other carefully placed locations lay couches and stands made of marble with lamps lit at every marble column making the room glow even though it wasn't night yet. "Wow." James said under his breath but Gellius heard him anyway.

"Impressive isn't it? This atrium is my favorite room. I have a friend that had to leave Rome and he gave me the domus. By the way, you never did tell me your names."

"That is even more impressive that he would give you his domus. My name is James and this is Red."

Gellius' cocked an eyebrow. "Unusual names for someone of your position. And truth be told, I am watching it until he returns. If he ever does, of which I have my doubts." He guided them to a doorway at the rear of the atrium and up a raised platform into another room. He gestured to a couch while sitting on a well padded marble chair with elegantly carved legs. "Please sit, what is mine is yours tonight."

"Thank you," James said sitting with Red joining him, "and what can I say, we like to be unique. What happened to your friend? I can't imagine him wanting to up and leave everything."

"Well ..." Gellius paused looking around, "he didn't want to. He was accused of trading directly, and being a member of the Senate, that, as you know, is strictly forbidden. I know he didn't do it, but rather than risk losing everything to the state he quietly gave it to me and left with the hope of returning to clear his name later on."

"I see, so you are keeping it for him then?"

"Yes, and if he returns, everything will be almost as he left it. To be honest, I wouldn't mind if he did. This place is a little large for me." Gellius said as a stout woman in worn but well maintained clothing sporting fresh food stains poked her head around the doorway.

"Master? What would you like for tonight's cena?"

"Zoe! Come in! You needn't hide around the corner." Gellius said waving his arm for her to join them.

Zoe bowed her head lower. "Master, you know that does not make me comfortable."

"Well no reason it should when I tell you to. As for the cena, how about chicken, bread, apples, and figs?"

"I will make whatever you wish. I thought perhaps you might want something else more extravagant for your guests?"

"They are friends not senators, I am not trying to impress them," Gellius said with a wave of his hand.

"And we have imposed enough by being here tonight. We do not need anything but a simple meal," James said.

Zoe nodded. "I understand Master. I do have everything, I shall begin at once. I wish to thank you for the new vent it makes the culina so much nicer."

"As I said before, you are very welcome. Besides, it is in my best interest if you can see."

Zoe bowed again. "Yes it is. Nonetheless, I thank you," she said backing out of the room.

Red looked towards Gellius and gave him a quizzical look. "So she could see?"

Gellius laughed. "Well she spends all day long in the culina cooking. The problem is, that generates a lot of smoke and often it is hard to see being the room is small. I had a tube put in the roof so the smoke could escape."

"That was very nice of you."

"It is in my best interest if she can cook better. Not to mention the smoke would often spread to the rest of the domus."

"If I may ask, why didn't she want to come in here with us?" James said.

"Her previous Master was a hard man and beat her for the simplest annoyance or mistake. I rescued her before he could kill her. She is an amazing cook, and Greek even. How he could beat that wonderful woman is a mystery. I am surprised he was willing to sell her to me, but I am grateful he did."

James looked around and leaned closer in his chair which squeaked slightly with the shifting in weight. "Can I ask you something else?"

"Yes?"

"Who were the two men that joined you in the tepidarium?"

Gellius' face lost some color. "You saw that?"

Red nodded. "Yes we did. What did they want?"

"They are … associates of mine. They wanted me to do something for them. And at first I agreed. It was to help the Rome after all. Something any citizen is willing to do."

"What did they want you to do?"

Gellius sat back in his chair and let out a deep sigh. "As you know, our republic is threatened, and some say dead, because of Caesar. Because of this, many feel his removal will restore

Rome. The problem is, the only reliable way to do that is to kill him."

James got up and looked around outside the doorway then sat back down. "And they wanted you to kill Caesar?"

Gellius sighed again. "Yes."

"And?" Red asked.

"I agreed. It was for the good of Rome. Caesar often comes to me for treatment so it would have been easy to give him something that did the opposite of the expected outcome. But when I talked with you earlier today, I realized my mistake. I am a doctor! Pledged to do no harm! There must be a better way to do this. Caesar is one man, we can have him removed if we join together."

"And the others do not agree with you?" Red said.

Gellius ran his fingers through his thinning hairline then rubbed his neck. "Yes. They feel there is no other choice and I should hold up my end of the agreement."

James shifted again in the hard chair. "I can see your problem. And I agree, there must be a better way."

"I wish my associates did."

Thaleia appeared in the doorway and bowed low. "Master, the triclinium is ready. Zoe said the chicken will be done soon."

"Thank you Thaleia. We will be there in a moment. Please be there, ready for us."

Thaleia bowed lower. "Of course Master." She said before turning and disappearing in the other direction.

"Come my friends, our cena awaits," Gellius said standing. A moment later they were in an elaborately decorated room. Mosaics covered the floor in elegant patterns, the walls contained impressive frescoes and even more detailed paintings further adored the room.

In the middle a large table surrounded by three couches elongated and inclined near the table which could hold three people each. The table contained bread, figs, apples and several bottles. "I know it is just the three of us, so you may have a lectus to yourself if you wish."

"Very gracious of you." Red said as they lay down on the couches so their feet pointed away from the table and still could easily reach the food. A moment later Thaleia appeared with a large bowl of water and began to wash Gellius' feet and hands. Then moved on to James.

"Oh I can–" James caught Red's stare and Thaleia's perplexed look. "But I will, of course let you do it." Thaleia bowed and removed James' sandals, washed his feet then continued to his hands. Then repeated the process on Red.

Gellius grabbed several figs from the table and popped them into his mouth. "I always love figs, especially this time of year. I think they get too sweet later in the season."

James took one and managed to not make a disagreeable face. "Yes very good."

Dinner continued without much conversation. And after most of the apples and figs were gone Zoe appeared with a plate of steaming meat. She bowed slightly as she placed the plate in the middle of the table so everyone could reach it. "Enjoy. If you need anything more, let me know." Then backed out of the room.

As the meal progressed, several times Thaleia mixed the wine to each person's tastes. Gellius' eyebrow raised when he saw how weak their wine was. "My friends you are missing out, with having so much water in your wine. I can assure you it is of top quality."

Red smiled. "Oh it has nothing to do with quality, we cannot have much without effects."

"I do not think I have seen citizens drink wine so thin, even slaves drink stronger beer. But of course you know your limits," Gellius said with a slight shrug.

Thaleia or another slave continually washed everyone's hands as they ate. While Red and James felt odd about having their hands washed by someone else, they did not want to appear anymore unusual in Gellius' eyes.

After the meal was done Thaleia and several other slaves cleared the table. "Thaleia, tell Zoe she did a wonderful job as always." Gellius said patting his extended middle.

"I will Master. Will you be needing anything else?"

"Are the extra cubiculum's ready for my guests?"

"Yes they are. The beds have been made and the lamps lit."

"Then you may rest for the evening. I will call you if I need."

Thaleia bowed low. "Very well Master." She turned on her heel and walked out of the triclinium.

"You treat your slaves well." James said when Thaleia was out of earshot.

Gellius shifted position on his couch then sat up. "Well I have had most of them for many years. And I always felt if they are treated well, then they will be more loyal and watch out for you rather than stab you in the back at the first opportunity."

"Sounds like a good method," James said as he sat up.

"It does allow me to sleep well at night. I don't know how others do it when most of your slaves want to kill you if they get the chance. Your cubiculums are down the hall to the right of the peristylium. The cool air from the garden should help you sleep."

Red nodded. "I am sure it will."

"If you both will excuse me, I must get some rest. I have an early day at the Circus Maximus tomorrow."

"Oh?"

"Yes, there is a great race going on tomorrow and I know several people on the blue team. You both are welcome to join me if you wish."

James inclined his head. "Thank you, yes we would."

"Than I shall see you in the morning. Sleep well." Gellius said as he stood and walked out of the triclinium.

Red and James also stood and headed down the hall in a similar direction. On their right they found several small bedrooms, two were open with oil lamps illuminating the interior with their flickering glow. "How about this one?" James said pointing to the nearest room.

Red shrugged. "Fine with me."

Atrus beeped softly. "Sir, may I remind you that in this time-zone men and women generally did not sleep together."

"Then I will take the other room," Red said.

"Atrus, that may be, but we are going to make an exception in this case."

Red raised an eyebrow. "Oh we are?"

"Yes I do not think it is a good idea for both of us to sleep at the same time. This way we can in shifts. Besides, I don't want to leave you alone in this place."

"While that is sweet of you, you do realize that there are bars on the windows and the door is very thick. I'm sure I will be fine."

"I have no doubt love, but I still think it is a better idea if one of us stays awake."

Red leaned close and kissed his lips. "I am sure you do. But I will be fine, and it is not worth Gellius thinking us anymore unusual than he already does."

James sighed. "All right, all right. But I reserve the right to check on you."

"You are so sweet, you know that?" Red said kissing his lips again before heading into her own bedroom and shutting the large door.

James sighed. "Atrus how is your power level?"

"Adequate. I can be on for most of the night before I need to recharge."

"Good I want you to monitor Red. If anything out of the ordinary happens with her or this house I want you to tell me immediately."

"Acknowledged."

James entered the other bedroom, shut the heavy door, and looked around. The floor was decorated in detailed mosaics as in the rest of the house. Wonderful paintings filled the walls with color. At the other end of the small room laid a single bed with pulled back linen sheets. The oil lamp flickered as a small breeze blew through the iron barred window. James sat on the bed and found it much more comfortable than it looked. He took his bag that was carefully hidden under his toga, slid it under the bed, lay down, and watched the shadows from the oil lamp dance across the detailed ceiling in the same pattern as the floor.

James tried to stay awake but after a while his eyelids became extremely heavy. A moment later his eyes cracked open like rusty hinges as they focused on Atrus' hologram.

"Sir! Finally, you are awake."

"Atrus? What's going on?" James said with a slight slur as

he sat up. Light pouring from the window meant it was well past sunrise.

"I have been trying to wake you for some time. I cannot locate Red."

"WHAT!" James said jumping to his feet, which felt like rubber and his knees buckled. He sat back down on the bed before he fell over. "What do you mean you can't find her? You were to monitor us at all times and wake me if anything unusual happened."

"Sir, I know that. But if you recall, I told you I did not have quite enough power to stay online for the whole night. At one point I had to shut down for fifteen minutes to flash charge which then gave me enough power for the rest of the night. However, when I came back online, Red was no longer in scanning range. I have been trying to wake you since that time."

James stood up then felt a little light-headed and sat back down again. "How long have you been trying to wake me?"

"Four hours, ten minutes."

"Four hours!? I wasn't that tired. You should have been able to wake me."

"Sir if I may suggest removing me and allowing an intensive scan."

"Agreed." James said removing Atrus from his holster, held him out, and closed his eyes. A thin green beam lanced out from the tip, traveling up and down James' entire body several times before it retracted.

"I think I understand. I am detecting an unusual herbal compound in your system."

"What? Someone drugged me?"

"I suspect both of you. As it would have made it much easier to take Miss Red unconscious or otherwise incapacitated. In summary, I believe the phrase is someone slipped you the Roman equivalent of knock out drops or as you might call it, a Mickey Finn."

James shook his head and blinked several times to clear the cobwebs. "Whoa, I think you are right. But why didn't it affect us sooner?"

"The concoction was far less potent than in your time-line."

James shook his head again, grabbed his bag from under the bed, and forced himself to his feet. Each step to the door was easier and by the time he actually opened it, the world had stopped spinning. He went over to Red's room, found the door unlocked, slipped inside, and looked around. It was as Atrus had thought, with no sign of a struggle, she must have been taken in her sleep.

He found her backpack under the bed and slipped it inside his linen bag. "Someone took her for sure, she would have never left this. Let alone not tell us." A moment later he was standing outside of Gellius' room pounding on the door.

A sleepy-eyed Gellius opened the door. "What is all the pounding for?"

"Red is missing!"

Gellius' eyes shot open the rest of the way. "What do you mean she is missing? She is not in her room?"

"No. And she is not in the domus either or I would not have bothered you."

Gellius stood out in the hallway and shouted "Thaleia! Jovinus! Come here! *Now!*"

A moment later Thaleia appeared in a different toga than yesterday and Jovinus was wearing the same armor as before. It was Jovinus that spoke first. "Yes Sir? What is the matter?"

"James said Red is missing. Have either of you seen her?"

They both shook their heads. "I only got up a short while ago. She is not in her room?" Thaleia asked.

"No she is not. Jovinus, how could anyone get past you? Weren't you guarding the whole night?" James asked glaring at the man as he shifted uncomfortably from one sandaled foot to another.

"I was for most of the night. But as it got late, I shut and bolted the front door securing the domus as I normally do. I did not think it would be a problem."

"No one is accusing you Jovinus," Gellius said.

"Yes, I'm only trying to find her. Did you see anything out of the ordinary?"

"Well ..." Jovinus said stroking his chin. "The lock on the front door was turned in a different direction than I usually do. But I thought I had done it differently last night. I was falling asleep when I locked it." Jovinus' eyes fell. "I am sorry Sir, I have failed you. And with one of your guests."

Gellius took a hold of Jovinus' shoulder. "You have not failed me. The door is as you left it otherwise? That means someone would have had to let Red out."

"Or someone let in to take her. How many people have a key?"

"Only I and Gellius have one." Jovinus said producing a heavy iron key from a pouch on his hip.

Gellius sighed. "That is not quite true." He said looking to Thaleia who's eyes quickly shot down to the ground "Thaleia, I gave you one the other day so you could go early to the market, and you have not returned it."

"I ... I ... I ... "

"Thalia, what have you done?"

Thaleia pulled out an iron key and placed it in Gellius'

hand. "I am sorry Master. I am so sorry. But I did not want you to be harmed!"

"Harmed? Why would I be harmed?"

Thaleia sunk to her knees and clutched Gellius' short cloak. "They said you would be hurt if I didn't do as they asked."

Gellius' shoulders slumped. "I never thought they would go this far."

"The people you told us about last night?" James asked.

"Yes. I thought they would find someone else or another way. But to do this ..."

"Never mind that, it is done. Thaleia, what exactly did they say?"

Her voice trembled, and she never looked up. "They mentioned Circus Maximus and that they would meet you there today after you did what you agreed to," she went lower to the ground, if that was even possible, "Master please forgive me."

Gellius looked down at Thaleia, "You did what you thought best to ensure my safety. The choice you made was wrong, but I understand the loyalty behind it. If we get Red back, I shall forget this whole incident."

"Oh thank you Master!" Thaleia said as she looked up her face streaked with tears.

"Gellius, please go to the Circus Maximus as they instructed." James said in a stern voice.

"What? I am sorry but I will not do what they ask, even if it is to save Red."

James shook his head. "I am not saying that you should, only that you go to Circus Maximus and appear that the mission is complete. You mentioned going today anyway, I assume you have a regular location you go to?"

"Yes, I have a reserved box. But what will that accomplish?"

"It will give me time to find her."

Gellius' eyes widened. "Find her? In all of Rome?"

"No, I suspect they will have her at Circus Maximus as well."

"Even so there will be 150,000 citizens there today, how can you find her in all of that?"

"You leave that to me. All you have to do is go there and act as though everything is going according to their plan."

Jovinus spoke up. "I will go with you. It is also my fault your lady was taken."

"It is not your fault, and I would feel better if you go with Gellius and take Thaleia as well so they think everything is normal."

"But I don't normally join him at the races."

"Perhaps not; however, he may need your protection and I will feel better if you are with him. Understood?"

"Very wise. I shall guard him with my life."

"Of that I have no doubt," James said.

They waited several hours before leaving to give the appearance that Gellius did create the poison and delivered it as instructed. Approaching the giant Circus Maximus, James went off in a different direction and impressed upon them to act naturally and show that everything was going according to plan.

The streets were getting crowded but James located a side street that only had a few people at the one end. "Atrus?" he whispered while standing in the corner of a not-yet-open bakery.

"Yes Sir?"

"Is there anyway we can locate Red?"

"I could do an intensive scan, but that would alert everyone to my presence."

"No we can't have that. Hmm, could we locate her A.T.E. instead?"

"And how do you propose we do that? I could do a scan, but that would not be any different from scanning for Red herself."

James looked around and still didn't see anyone. "You did software updates to them, could you initialize hers to send out a beacon we could locate?"

"Sir, I need to have touching proximity to do that kind of update. However, I could send out an update pulse which the A.T.E should respond, but it will be a very low intensity signal. Normally I would not be able to locate the origin of such a weak signal, but with the reduced electromagnetic radiation of this time-line it may be possible."

"How far can the pulse reach?"

"I can only give a rough estimate since I have never done this before, perhaps half the size of the Circus Maximus."

"So, if we get almost to the center of it, you might be able to detect the ping from Red anywhere in the building?"

"Yes Sir, again in rough theoretical estimation. However, I could expand that range if I use the Shell. It can send and detect pulses just as well as I. It will also make tracking the responses from the A.T.E. easier."

"All right, we will do that once inside." James said as he continued walking joining the crowds heading towards the immense stadium that was the Circus Maximus.

Thoughts of Red and what he would do if she was harmed flooded his mind, which he quickly pushed back. "No, I will not allow myself to fall down that pit, she is all right. I will make sure of it," he muttered.

Red opened her heavy eyelids to two large men smiling.

"Ah good you are awake." She tried to sit up, but they pushed her back down onto the stone floor. "Stay there."

"Who ... who are you?" She said while shaking her head trying to clear the cobwebs. Looking down her hands were tied, but they didn't remove her toga so at least they didn't take advantage of her.

"That is not of your concern. You are our guest for now."

She shook her head again fighting to concentrate. She knew that feeling all too well, someone had drugged her last night. It was the only explanation how these men could have taken her so easily. "And for how long?"

"That depends on your friend Gellius."

"On Gellius?" she repeated, "why?"

"That is not of your concern. Keep quiet and you will be free soon enough," he drew a sword from its sheath and held it to her neck, "cause us any problems and you won't see them again. Understood?"

Red felt the cold metal against her neck. "Perfectly. Can I at least sit up now? My back hurts."

The one man looked to the other and after some contemplation, he nodded. Red inched herself up with the sword still poised at her throat and her back complained even more loudly than before. She looked around the large concrete structure. Light was streaming in around the columns and in the distance she could see a large oval shaped opening in the roof.

Moving a little to get a better view she could see the floor of the oval area was dirt with center posts that stretched almost the full-length. Squinting she could see that encircling the whole area were seating for spectators. A great many of them already filled with people. She realized this must be Circus

Maximus, nothing else of this massive size could be in this time-zone.

Looking around the column her back was against, she realized they must be on the far end of the building, just above the ground floor. Indicating whoever was behind this had a lot of money. No one was around except for the two sizable brutes on either side of her. Shouting wouldn't do any good, not to mention the less contamination of the time-line, the better. She considered making a run for it, but her thoughts were still too sluggish for moving at full speed. Sighing, she sat back and watched as the crowds continued to fill the building.

James entered one of the large arched passageways into the main spectator section of Circus Maximus. He made his way through the crowds until he reached the seats closest to the dirt track. He then ducked into a lower supporting section that gave him cover. Removing the Shell from his bag, he powered it on and held it out. "Okay Atrus, it is online," he whispered.

"Acknowledged. I have control. Hover systems online and engaging the holographic cloak." He said as the Shell disappeared. "I am deploying it on the other side of this structure from our position. Between that location and this one, it should give us the coverage we require to–"

"Just do it! We can't waste any time. If these people suspect a trick–"

"I am well aware of the situation Sir. The Shell has reached the optimum location. Sending ping."

"Anything?"

"Yes, to the left of our position on the farthest edge of the loop and one level below us."

"Below? I thought this was the lowest?"

"There is one more level, it would appear to be for maintenance or needing to move materials out of sight of the general public."

"That may work to our advantage. How do we get down there?"

Atrus displayed a small holographic map. "As you can see there is an entrance door fifty meters from our position."

James nodded and walked as quickly as he could without drawing attention. A few minutes later he found a locked door that led below. Looking around and finding no one in the area he took out the gun and prepared to blast the lock.

Atrus appeared causing him to take a step back. "Geeze Atrus! What is it?"

"Sir if I may make a suggestion of changing the gun to a sonic setting of 4452, I believe it will have the effect we require without destroying the lock ... or the door itself."

James opened the control panel in the grip, keyed in a few commands on the touch screen and snapped it shut. "This had better work," he said muttering while pulling the trigger.

A cone of almost invisible energy erupted from the barrel and the door shook but remained in place.

"That did a lot of good didn't it?" James said as he pulled open the grip control setting it back to a high power level.

"Why not push on it before you go and vaporize the whole thing?"

James nudged the door with his foot and it creaked open revealing the entrance to the darker, lower section. "Well I'll be, it worked. What exactly was that setting?"

"A sonic disruption that moved the tumblers into the proper position and unlocked the door as a result."

"Nice. Where is the Shell?" Just as he spoke the Shell appeared in front of him.

"Right there."

"Sheesh warn me next time, will you? I could have run into it."

"I wouldn't have let you do that."

"Sure you wouldn't." James muttered as he went down the steps, closing the door after, and replacing the gun under his toga. The crowd above roared as several of the racing teams appeared. But no one seemed to be in on this level.

James passed several open seating areas very close to the track with wonderful views of the racing teams. Many of the elegantly covered chairs were moved back under the overhang, but they were all unoccupied. "I thought you said this was for maintenance? These must be some of the most expensive seats."

"I based my analysis on the harder to access location, and the lack of people. It is possible that these seats are reserved and no one is making use of them yet."

"All of them? That seems very unusual."

"I agree, but for the moment it is the only possibility I can come up with," Atrus stated.

James moved carefully from area to area nearing the point Atrus had shown him previously. "How much farther?" James whispered.

"Two more sections."

James saw them.

Two very large men on either side of Red, her back was to a large column and one of them held a sword to her throat. "Atrus I am going to need your help. We need to take out both men at the same time. I don't want Red hurt, and not to mention I don't want them to see anything of us."

"Acknowledged. Stun I assume?"

"Yes I will take the guy with the sword. You get the other one."

The Shell hovered into position. "I have a lock."

"Okay, on my mark …three …two …one …mark." Twin lances of energy lashed out and struck both men instantaneously. For a second nothing happened. Then the sword fell from the man's grip, clanging on the concrete as both men went down in a heap.

Red looked around but didn't see anything but the two men going unconscious. Then James appeared from behind a large support. "James!"

"Hello love, miss me?" James said as he walked over and started untying the crude ropes. The Shell hovered along behind him.

"Always. Now can you tell me what the heck happened?"

James finished removing the ropes and helped her to her feet. "The same people that tried to have Gellius poison Caesar thought they could use you as a bargaining chip and get him to go through with it."

"But how did they do it? I think I was drugged with something."

James nodded as she wobbled a bit on her feet. "Yes they got us both, but I think you had more than I."

"But how? We all drank and ate the same thing."

"Thaleia. They promised to kill or otherwise harm Gellius and she did it to protect him. She obviously slipped in something extra when mixing the wine."

Red leaned on James but she was improving with every

step. "That makes sense. How did you know where to find me?"

"A hunch. They told Gellius to meet them here after the deed was done. I figured they would want to keep things as simple as possible rather than have you stashed somewhere else then brought here. And I was right."

They reached the stairs and slipped back through the same door as before. Red felt almost normal and was leaning on James a little less every minute. "It seems odd this whole level is unused. It looks like the best seats."

James nodded. "I know, it doesn't make sense."

Red stopped as her eyes flashed. "Unless all the senators are behind this. They would have the prestige for such seats."

"Then the poisoning attempt was not by someone new, it is part of history. A part we didn't know."

Red nodded. "Right, they tried it, and when it failed, they grew more desperate and resorted to an alternate plan of stabbing him to death."

"So we helped along history again. Unless they continue to go after Gellius."

"I doubt that. Those men will be too embarrassed to report to anyone. It would mean their lives. They will simply disappear. And since we know Caesar is killed tomorrow, they don't have time to do anything else but what history records," Red said giving James a squeeze. Then her eyes went wide. "My pack! It is still under my bed at Gellius' domus!"

James smiled and pulled her pack from under his toga. "Well it is a good thing I picked it up then."

"Oh I love you!" Red said kissing him.

"And I love you," he said kissing her back, "shall we warp out of here while all of Rome is watching the races?"

Red shook her head. "No, we need to at least tell Gellius he is safe and they won't come after him again. Otherwise he might go looking for us and the less of a temporal footprint we make the better."

"Agreed. Atrus? Where is Gellius?"

Atrus appeared before them. "I anticipated your request and used the Shell to locate them. They are one level above and near the front. And before you ask, I made sure no one was in the area before I activated my hologram." He smiled as his image winked out.

About thirty minutes later they found Gellius cheering on the blue team along with Thaleia. Jovinus stood watch and noticed their approach. "Sir, we have guests," Jovinus said with a smile.

Gellius turned around and grinned. "It is good to see you Red. I see James found you as he suspected. Did everything go well?"

James nodded. "Yes and you will be pleased to know that they will not bother you again."

"How can you be so sure?"

"Oh we can be, trust us," Red said with her most confident smile.

"My friends I do. You have done much for me, and I am most grateful. You are welcome to stay for as long as you wish. Or any time you are in Rome."

"We thank you, but we must be on our way."

"I understand. Then until we meet again," Gellius said extending his hand.

James grasped it firmly. "Until then. Thank you for everything."

"No, it is I who thank you," he said smiling.

It was early evening by the time they reached an area near

the edges of the city large enough to use. "Think this will do?"

Red felt of the ground. "Yes this will work. Let me change first. I can't warp in this." She said pulling the toga over her head.

"Atrus? Anyone in range?"

Atrus appeared before them. "Negative. And may I suggest you store the Shell?" Atrus said as the Shell's cloak deactivated. "It is nearly out of power by using the cloak for so long."

"And it may get tossed about when Red opens the warp."

"Yes, that too."

The Shell floated down into James' hand, the hidden compartment opened, and he tapped the power control. The compartment resealed as he slipped the Shell into his pack. He looked back at Red who had already changed into her bodysuit. "That was fast. You just didn't want to let me watch you strip."

She walked up and rubbed her hips with his. "You can watch later. I for one want to get out of this time-zone."

"I am going to hold you to that," James said with a grin.

"Promises promises."

"And I keep my promises." James said as he pulled off his toga revealing the white shirt underneath, slid into his black pants, then replaced the sandals with his matching padded support shoes. "Oh does that feel better. I was getting tired of those sandals."

Red lowered herself into a sprinting position. "Ready?"

James stuffed the toga and sandals into his pack. "Ready."

"Let's do this!" Red said as she bolted in a clockwise direction faster and faster. The air swirled detaching leaves from nearby trees. Small twigs and other debris joined to follow along in her wake. She pushed a little more and a lightning bolt hit the ground ripping open a crack in the very essence of space and time. She pushed again, and it opened further then shrank back to a mere crack.

"Red? Is there something wrong?" James shouted over the maelstrom.

"It is happening again! I don't know if I can hold it."

"I can help!" He said pulling out the gun.

"No! Don't you dare! I can do this!"

She pushed for all she was worth and the warp opened just big enough for a person to pass through. "James go NOW!"

He ran for the warp and dove in with Red behind him a millisecond later.

In the distance a man wearing armor stood his mouth agape. When he could finally shut it again, he headed back to Gellius to let him know he was certain they would not be back tonight.

$$-\ 10\ -$$

The air swirled around the stone floor. Ornate carvings shook as a spark flashed ripping open a fracture in the very essence of space and time. It quickly grew into an angry mass of convoluted energy before finally spreading out into a rough diamond shape. James crashed out of the warp hitting the stone floor with a large thud. Red fell out right after him. The warp as usual, quickly receded and disappeared into nothingness plunging the room into darkness.

"Ouch!" James said rubbing his knee. "We would have to land on a stone floor."

"I know," Red said rubbing her hip, "but you wanted to jump."

"No, you said you could do it. I was willing to wait, or give you some help," James said with a hidden wink.

"Well, I for one wanted to get out of there before we did any more damage to the time-line. It was too risky staying."

"Oh, I agree. But I noticed it was not a normal jump … again"

Red rubbed her neck. "I know. Felt like we hit something in the warp. It must have been Keleeigan again. But I don't understand how. The other times should be behind us, temporally speaking."

"Are you sure?" James said.

Red's eyes widened. "Atrus?! Did you detect anything unusual in the warp?"

Atrus' hologram flashed into existence lighting the large room. "There was another large spike in the temporal field and we apparently intersected with it."

"Why didn't you mention this before?"

"I thought it was a normal fluctuation."

"Atrus, have you ever seen that particular fluctuation before?"

"No."

"And how many jumps have we been on?"

"Well it depends on if you count–"

"A lot, right?"

"Yes."

"And you never saw this particular fluctuation before right?"

"That is correct."

"Then in this case it is not *normal*!"

"Acknowledged. I had assumed it was commonplace even though I had not personally experienced it with you. I apologize for my error, and I will not do so again."

"Good, now what was it?"

"I have checked my reviewed my data on the time in question, and upon further examination I believe I can concur with James' previous hypothesis: it was indeed Professor Keleeigan."

James sat down in a nearby stone chair. "How is that possible? You said he should be behind us temporally speaking."

"I don't know, it doesn't make any sense. Unless we caught

up to him again in the warp, even though we shouldn't have," Red said still rubbing her sore hip.

Atrus nodded. "I suspect that is what happened. It is also possible that as his power supply dwindles further, the field becomes even more erratic taking unusual paths. Perhaps even several paths through the temporal stream. Magnified by the failed attempt to stabilize the field earlier."

"Agreed. Now Atrus where are we?" James asked sucking in a breath of stale musty air.

"A underground chamber of some sort. That much I have been able to ascertain."

"This area seems large, but we can't see very far," Red said looking around, "Atrus can you light up this area?"

"For a short period. For a longer one I would require assistance from the Shell. It should have recharged enough to do so."

"Hang on, might as well use it," James said pulling the Shell out and activating it, "no sense in draining your power reserve when we don't need to."

The Shell levitated off of James' hand as Atrus nodded. "Stand by, activating holo projection." A large ball of light appeared in the air driving shadows from the room. They stood there with mouths agape. Just beyond them laid rivers of liquid with some sort of ornate box in the middle of the large area. Above it jewels were set into the ceiling giving the appearance of constellations. The silver liquid moved around as if pumped. Other areas looked like land.

James blinked. "That looks like an overhead map of China. What is the liquid?"

Atrus' eyes narrowed. "Mercury, and a lot of it. It also seems to be circulated by some kind of pump system. Quite fascinating."

"Mercury! Wow why would anyone build a map with mercury for water?"

Red's eyes widened. "Oh no. Atrus can you scan the ornate box in the center?"

"Yes, deploying Shell." The Shell hovered over and a green beam shot out running over the object up and down several times before retracting and the Shell hovered back over. "Projecting my findings." Atrus said as an exact copy of the object hung in the air. "It seems to be a coffin or sarcophagus, but unlike any I have encountered before. There are several safeguards in place that if activated will trigger hidden spikes in the surrounding floor to shoot up killing anyone standing in the area."

"Is there a body inside it?"

"Yes, he has been dead for approximately two years."

James pointed to a large plate on the side. "Can you read this?"

"Yes. 'Here lies our Sovereign Emperor Qin Shi Huang who shall live forever in the next world.'"

"Huang? This is his tomb? How the heck did we end up here?"

Red sighed. "We knew that warp wasn't stable, and it obviously intersected with Keleeigan again sending us off course. This is not good at all."

"Well other than being in a dead guy's tomb with enough mercury to poison a whole country, how can it get any worse?"

"The unstable nature of his jumps are making it difficult for *us* to jump! Which are getting progressively worse. We need to catch and stop him next time. Or we may not have another chance."

"You won't be able to open another warp?"

"Well I might be able to open one, but to actually get somewhere is another situation entirely. Remember I tried to follow Keleeigan into 210 AD, but we end up around 175 BC, then Rome 44 BC, only to fall backwards to 208 BC? That is one heck of a temporal mess up, considering that I am using the crystal and normally have pinpoint accuracy with it." Red pointed to her headband.

The hologram of the sarcophagus disappeared. "It is rather disconcerting," Atrus said.

"Which part?" James sneered, "the part where we are in the tomb of a dead emperor, which I assume is still sealed considering nothing here is touched. Or the part that we may not be able to jump out of here?"

"Both," Red said, "however, I think we can jump from this tomb at least. Atrus, could part of the original problem be that we jumped twice at the same location that Keleeigan did?"

Atrus nodded. "I suppose that can be part of the equation. But the unpredictability of the Keleeigan's temporal field makes being certain an impossibility."

"Great," James said getting to his feet. "Sounds like fun. We might die here or the next jump." He started walking off to towards the large doorway to their right.

"Where are you going?"

"To check this place out. Might as well since we are stuck here for the moment."

"If you think you are leaving me here, you got another thing coming!" Red said running after him and locking her arm around his. The Shell's high intensity holographic light shut down and a lower, smaller one materialized in front of it, then moved to light the corridor beyond.

"Thanks Atrus," James said.

"You are welcome Sir."

On either side of the long passageway were ornate stone carvings and paintings showing the life of the emperor. "This is amazing. I don't think this tomb was ever opened, at least not intact."

"Why not?" James asked.

"I am not sure. I do recall the location being found, but they never actually opened it. At least not officially. It may have been ransacked long before your time, but it was never opened to prove one way or the other. Atrus? Do you know anything more?"

Atrus walked beside them. "Not much. The tomb's location was found; however, due to fear of being unable to preserve its contents, opening was deemed too problematic. Areas around the tomb were excavated revealing a great deal about Huang and China of the time. Eventually the technology was developed to explore the tomb safely. However, with the radioactive incidents and the resulting nano plague after, all interest in such things were abandoned."

"Well that was in your original time-line. Don't tell me you didn't peek at history as it unfolded, without the world dying." James said with a smile.

"I did. However, I did not specifically look to see if any details on Qin Shi Huang's tomb had changed. I was more interested in other aspects of how history unfolded."

James looked at Red and grinned. "I have a feeling it will be the first thing he looks up when we get back there."

Red laughed. "No bets here."

At the end of the long corridor they found many dead bodies. Some were male others female. The women outnumbered the men by a large margin. "Well these people don't look like they stole anything. I wonder why they are here."

"Legend says that many people were buried with the emperor. Concubines, officials, and builders to maintain the secrecy of his tomb. Although I doubt the concubines were to guarantee that. They probably didn't have a clue until the doors were sealed behind them," Red said.

"Which begs the question, someone had to close the doors, and had the know-how to do it. Therefore, someone knew the tombs secrets and walked away."

"A impressive show of logic Sir," Atrus said.

"Thank you Atrus. But this brings up another question. How much air is down here as the tomb still appears to be sealed."

"Good question," Red said.

Atrus closed his eyes as if in thought. "From the size of the map room, and some of these other chambers, I suspect you have over two days. Possibly more."

They turned and went down another smaller corridor. "Well at least we don't have to be in a hurry."

Red shook. "Speak for yourself. I want to get out of here as soon as possible."

James smiled. "You and me both. I just figured it was better that we don't have to leave within the hour or suffocate."

Red nodded. "True."

When they reached the end of the smaller corridor, it opened up into a large room filled with all manners of food. Wine, rice, pots filled with other editable concoctions. "Wow I didn't think they buried food with their dead like the Egyptians."

Red shook her head. "They didn't normally. Probably something new that Huang did."

James jerked a thumb towards the corridor. "I am surprised

that the people back there didn't help themselves to some of this."

"I doubt they could see after the tomb was sealed and died trying to get someone to open the door."

"Perhaps, but wouldn't you try to feel around?"

"Yes … true … it doesn't make sense. Let's take a closer look at those bodies."

They walked back along the smaller corridor and found the bodies as they left them. "Atrus, do a scan, what did they die of?"

A green beam shot out from the hovering Shell running up and down each desiccated body and retracting. "It would seem that is not an easy answer."

"What do you mean?"

"While all of these people had high levels of arsenic in their bodies, not all were killed by it. Some killed each other, probably out of fear, others died shortly after by the poison."

"Sounds like they did go willingly, were sealed in, but were poisoned beforehand so they could not do much damage in here."

Atrus nodded. "I agree, that appears to be what happened. Some panicked killing each other, in the end leaving a few that slowly died from the poison."

James pointed to another corridor. "Let's see what is down this hall."

Red sighed. "You know curiosity killed the cat."

"Well the cat in here has been dead for a long time. Might as well check this place out."

Red rolled her eyes. "All right. Then we head back to the main chamber and warp out of here?"

James smiled. "Deal."

They walked along the corridor also lavishly painted, this

time with scenes of the emperor's conquests. When they finally reached the end, a large door stood still sealed.

Atrus pointed. "Sir may I suggest caution? After all, traps were detected around the sarcophagus."

"Good idea, can you scan the interior?"

"I will attempt to do so." Atrus said as he guided the Shell closer. A green beam lanced out at the top of the doorway then slowly lowered until it reached the bottom. Then repeated several more times before retracting.

"It is difficult to say since this stone is thicker than the sarcophagus. However, the door seems to open on a pivot point in the middle. Push on either side and it should open. But may I suggest that both of you lay on the floor and push that way?" Atrus said pointing at the left side of the door.

Red looked perplexed. "Why? What else did you find?"

"I cannot be certain, but I think there may be a trap if you open the door all the way. There is a small anomaly near the ceiling of the door. It may be an activation system of some kind."

"Okay, a good reason to lay on the floor then. Unless it is something that comes up from the floor."

"Negative, this floor is solid stone. Of that I am certain."

"All right, let's give this a shot. Red lie down and stay there I will push."

"You think you can push that open by yourself?"

"I can, now get down."

Red rolled her eyes. "All right."

Red got down on the floor and James rested on his belly and reached out with his right hand pushing at one edge of the large door. Nothing happened. James moved up closer and pushed with both hands. Still nothing.

Red smirked. "So you can open it all by yourself can you?"

"Oh hush and give me a hand."

Red smiled and squeezed the backside that was so prominently displayed. "Only because you asked so nicely."

They both grunted and pushed and finally the door moved slightly. "We are getting it!"

"Remind me again why we are bothering?" Red grunted.

"Curiosity."

"And need I remind you what happened to the cat!" Red retorted.

Finally the large door pivoted on its center then swung the rest of the way from the inertia when they heard a slight click.

"What was–" James never had a chance to finish before a large bolt shot out of the room and over his head. It traveled through Atrus unabated causing his hologram to dissolve and reform, continuing on it reached more than halfway down the corridor before finally hitting the floor with a large clang. "Holy! Atrus, remind me to always take your suggestions."

Atrus bowed. "I will do so."

"Why do I get the feeling I am going to regret that?"

Red smiled and gave him another swat. "Perhaps because you will?"

They both stood up and peered in. One wall was covered with weapons of all kinds. Maces, spears, swords, crossbows, including hundreds if not thousands of arrows, all gleaming in the Shell's holographic light.

But when the light shifted to show the opposite wall, it caused them to gasp. Precious golden jewelry encrusted with the largest gemstones they ever saw covered the entire wall. Towards the center a large expertly crafted emerald measured more than a yard across and mounted flush into the wall.

Rubies encircled the large emerald stone with a golden area in-between the rubies and emerald.

There were even several long shenyi robes hanging in the corner that gleamed in the light from various precious jewel adornments sewn into the fabric along the sleeves and the entire length. Air currents from opening the door caused the robes to move creating facets reflecting off of the walls as if several old style disco balls were in the room.

"Wow," James whispered.

"Double wow, that must be the largest hunk of emerald crystal ever found," Red said.

"I thought they valued jade the most?"

"Well emerald is certainly harder to find, and it is similar in color to jade."

"True and wow look at that." James said pointing to a further corner of the large room. There sat a life size royal chariot made of solid jade, complete with green horses to pull it.

"Truly amazing. And even more so, they thought burying this would give him power in the next life. Well he did anyway."

"I can't imagine them finding this much jade, let alone carving it with such detail."

"Well keep in mind that if they didn't do a wonderful job, it probably meant their life was forfeit."

"Good point. Atrus are there any more traps? Can we get off of the floor now?"

The Shell moved forward slightly hovering its nose a centimeter inside the doorway and a green beam projected out touching everything in the room. "I detect several more traps in the room triggered either by the pressure on certain points in the floor, or by moving certain objects in the room. I believe it is safe for you to rise now. If you plan to explore the room further, I will need to guide you."

James shook his head as he stood and helped Red up. "No I think we have seen enough of that room." He said pushing the large stone door back into place. "After all, we have seen what no one else ever will. That is enough."

Red smiled. "You know there are moments like these that make me love you all the more."

James slipped his arm around Red's waist and squeezed. "Well then, since we have seen all the sights, shall we leave this place?"

"Sounds like a good idea to me." Red said as they started walking down the long corridor.

Halfway down as James stepped the floor gave slightly under his foot. "Wha–" He started to say as a bolt shot out of a hidden hole in the wall aimed directly at his chest. Atrus reacted immediately, and the Shell fired an intense energy beam from one of the twin retractable points on the otherwise smooth underside. The arrow vaporized into a white mist that flowed over James and Red. James eyes widened further. "Why didn't you tell me you could do that before!"

Atrus bowed. "I am sorry Sir, I was never certain my reaction time would be quick enough to offer the suggestion as a reliable option. Such a test is not worth risking your life."

Red squeezed him tightly knowing how close they were. "Thank you Atrus. Good shooting."

James sighed. "Yes Atrus thank you. But why didn't you tell me there were traps in this corridor?"

"I hadn't done an intensive scan of this corridor. We assumed that it would be free of traps, or that the traps would have already been tripped by those entombed with the emperor. The closed door indicated those traps would still be intact."

"Are there anymore?"

"Scanning now," Atrus said as another beam shot out of the front of the Shell covering the corridor from top to bottom before retracting, "you will be pleased to know that no further traps lie in this location."

James let out a deep breath he didn't know he was holding. "You got that right." He squeezed Red even tighter as they walked along back towards the center chamber. After a while they reached it with its mercury rivers and center bronze coffin. "Red, do you think you have enough room in here?"

"Well we don't have much of a choice do we? And I don't intend to spend my last days with Mr. Mercury." She said jerking a thumb towards the coffin.

"Agreed. We have to try it. Atrus bring down the Shell I should put it in my pack."

"Sir, if I may suggest that it be left out? You may have need of it."

"Have you forgotten how much wind Red generates when opening a warp? It would likely be thrown to the ground or smashed into the wall."

Atrus sighed and lowered the Shell into James' waiting hand. "You are of course correct." James opened the panel, deactivated the Shell, sealed the panel, and placed it in his pack. The only light in the room was from Atrus' projection. "Is there enough light? I can generate more for a short period."

Red stretched bending this way and that. "This is enough, we don't need to light this whole huge room since I am going to have to run in a tight circle anyway."

James paused raising a finger. "One problem I thought of.

Once I jump into the warp, this room is going to be very dark."

Red smiled. "You forget the warp itself generates some light, enough for me to see after you leave. Don't worry about it. I will be fine."

James' voice wavered several times. "Are you sure love?"

"Yes my darling. Remember I have done this for a long time before you tagged along."

"I know, I know. But I still worry."

Red walked over and kissed him on the lips. "I know and I love you for it. Now what do you say we blow this joint?"

James smiled. "I am all for that."

"Okay, let's do it!" Red said lowering into a sprinting position and bolted at high speed. The air in the room began to swirl faster and faster. The small amount of dust and dirt in the room started to follow Red in her wake. Red pushed a little more and a lightning bolt shot to the center and left an angry crack in its wake. Pushing further yet the warp opened, albeit reluctantly.

"Red what is wrong?"

"Still having problems like before, but not quite as bad." The warp grew a bit more but still was not large enough for someone to pass through.

"You can do it love! Just a little more!"

"I am trying! Okay here goes!" Red put on a large burst and the warp finally opened wide enough. But suddenly several metal bolts shot from the walls and the arrows followed Red in her wake.

"Atrus! Where did those arrows come from?"

"I don't know Sir! There must have been traps set into the walls and not triggered by the floors, I scanned them earlier!"

"Will you two shut it and JUMP! I can't keep this up!"

"Sorry love!" James shouted as he ran and jumped into the warp with Red right behind.

The warp twisted and pulled them in more directions than James could count. He looked back and saw Red's face flushed in concentration trying to guide them. The disturbance was getting worse. It felt as though they were being pushed back then pulled further ahead more than they were before only to be pushed back again. James reached back and found Red's hand and tried to concentrate. He managed to help before, and he would do it again. He had to.

He focused on Siberia and muttered 210 over and over again. He didn't see the rip in front of them form or both of them move towards it. Finally he felt as though they were being engulfed by a hungry force and crashed out and onto a soft patch of grass. He moved quickly flipping over, catching Red then pulling her down as an army of arrows that were right behind, zinged over their heads and hit the trees beyond.

He reached up and kissed her soft lips. "Whew that was a close one."

"Hmm? Yes it wass," she said her speech slightly slurred.

"Are you okay?"

"Really tired. Need to rest." She said placing her head on his shoulder and was fast asleep a second later.

"Atrus!"

"Yes Sir?"

"Is there anyone in the area?"

"Negative."

"Good, can we assume that Doc will arrive nearby? And anyway to tell how long that will be?"

"I do not detect any temporal signatures at the moment, therefore I will say he is not here. As to when he might arrive, if the current pattern remains true, he will arrive in a day or so. However, it could be longer that last jump was even more unconventional than previously experienced."

James rubbed his head. "No kidding. Okay, we will need a place to stay for the next day or so. Are there any caves in the nearby area?"

"Yes there is one to the north that should provide shelter."

"Good." James said as he pushed Red aside, got to his feet, then picked her up in his arms. "Lead the way."

Atrus appeared before him and pointed in the direction of the cave. "This way, and may I suggest that you deploy the Shell?"

"Why?"

"Well you are carrying Miss Red, if there is a problem I can be of more assistance if the Shell is online."

"How are the power reserves? Doesn't it need to recharge after all the use we gave it in the tomb?"

"It has about one eighth of normal capacity, which is a weeks worth of hovering around. If the holo system is used, or the weapons, then that will of course deplete it much quicker."

James nodded. "Of course. All right let me get it out." He carefully sat Red down, who never stirred, then removed the Shell from his bag, activated it, set it down, slung the bag back over his shoulder and carefully picked up Red. "Okay done."

The Shell rose up off of the ground and pivoted as it waited for them. Atrus pointed. "This way." He continued to walk alongside James as he struggled to carry Red and make his way across the country side. Several rock outcroppings forced him to go around as he couldn't climb them and carry Red. Finally, they reached the cave.

"Whew, I don't know if I could carry her much farther."

"Sir, I detect something in the cave."

"What? Someone is in there?"

"I am having difficulty determining that. Please stand by."

"Stand by? I just can't stand here and–" A large tiger appeared at the entrance to the cave. James' heart leapt into his throat as it growled.

"Oh my!" Atrus said as it raced towards him and passed directly through his projection causing it to flicker and reform. The tiger stopped, crouched, and looked at James with a mighty roar then jumped directly at him. James' eyes went wide.

A large energy bolt hit the tiger head-on causing him to freeze then a microsecond later incinerate into a white mist which blew away in the wind.

James took a breath, the first one since he saw the big cat. "Atrus, what took you so long?!"

"I am not sure Sir."

"Okay next time if you see a big tiger heading for us, and I have my hands full with Red, your orders are to shoot first and ask questions later. Got it?"

"Acknowledged. Warning! That last shot drained the Shell's power supply to a critical level. It will need to recharge as soon as possible."

James made his way to the cave and carefully set Red down as he moved his arms to shake the fatigue from them. "Okay bring it here." James said opening his hand. The Shell hovered down into his hand and he opened the panel, shut off the power supply, and sealed the panel again. He placed it back in his pack. "Atrus, is there anything else in this cave?"

"Negative, it does not reach that far back and nothing else is in the area."

"Good. I think I saw a broken tree not far from here that we can use for firewood. I suspect it is going to get cold tonight even though it is summer."

"You are correct, it will be uncomfortable at night without the use of a fire."

"Okay, I am going to get wood, you watch her while I do."

"And how can I tell you if something happens unless I am with you? And you already disabled the Shell so it can recharge."

"Right," James said placing Atrus back into the pocket of his holster, "we will keep close by and in scanning range. If Red needs us, we can be here in under a minute."

"That would work."

"Thank you Atrus," James said bowing slightly.

Atrus rolled his eyes. "There you go again."

"There what goes again?" James said in a mocking tone.

"Never mind Sir. Never mind."

James found a large log and pulled out his gun, activating one of the higher settings he fired several shots that blasted clean through cutting the log into several, manageable sections. He picked up what he could carry and made his way back to Red. He found her still asleep and made several more trips. James doubted they would need that much wood, but he didn't want her to get cold either.

He carefully made a pit at the entrance to the cave and encircled it with stones he could carry. With the stone circle completed he placed several logs in the middle, adjusted the power setting again, and blasted them in two locations.

The logs burned brightly. By now the sun had set, and the temperature dropped. He took out one of the expanding insulating blankets from his pack and covered Red. As she slept, he kept watch.

"Sir, I can wake you if anything occurs."

"And what are your power reserves at?"

"I have plenty Sir."

"We might need it later. Go into recharge."

"But Sir, I really think you should rest now."

"Atrus, go into recharge. I want you at full capacity, we may need it when Doc shows up."

"All right. Shutting down." Atrus said as his image faded and James heard a soft beep from his cylinder.

He stood at the entrance and watched the stars as they continued to grow in brightness. While sitting there he couldn't help but remember the stake out that went horribly wrong and almost cost him his agent status so soon after he got it. He wondered if it was going to be that way again. But he did make it out of that, and he would make it out of this. With Red *and* Doc.

He sat down and leaned back against the cave wall when he heard something stir. He spun around in with his knee in the dirt the gun drawn facing the sound.

Red coughed. "Hey point that somewhere else will you?"

James quickly put the weapon away. "Sorry love. We had an incident with a tiger earlier, and I guess I am a little on edge."

Red's eyes went wide as her skin tingled. "Tiger?"

"Yes one came out of this cave. I was holding you, but Atrus got it with the Shell. But, I guess my adrenaline is still on overdrive." He said walking over and sitting down beside her. "How are you feeling?"

"Better, still a little tired, but not bad. That jump was even worse than the last."

"I know, it felt like we were being bounced inside a pinball game. And I could see you were having trouble."

"No kidding, it fought me every time I tried to get here we were pulled back or pushed forward past this point."

"So we were being pushed around even more than Doc's lighthouse?"

Red nodded. "We were."

"Do you have any idea why?"

"If I were to hazard a guess, it is like I said before, due to Keleeigan's unstable temporal field it is having a toxic effect on the warp. If we don't stop it on this jump, I don't know if we can jump again."

"You mean we might be stuck here?"

"I hope not, but after that last one. It is looking that way. I felt you this time helping. If it wasn't for you, I don't know if we could have made it out."

James wrapped his arm around her. "I am here love, always. Anyway I can be, I will be."

Red smiled. "I know that. Still, it is always good to hear." She said softly kissing his cheek. "I am surprised Atrus hasn't said something by now."

"He is recharging."

"Did he get that low?"

"No, I figured he might need it later. And nothing going on now, and I couldn't sleep sooooo."

"So you took the first watch."

"Of a fashion." James said pulling out one of their energy bars, unwrapped it then handed it to Red, then did one for himself and pushed the dissolve tabs. The wrappers vanished into nothingness. "I am glad we don't have to worry about carrying empty wrappers around."

Red took a bite and munched. "Yes I always loved that feature of these. Are you sure we should be eating them?"

James shrugged. "We will get more after this jump, or we won't jump again by the sounds. Might as well use them and be ready for Doc when he shows up tomorrow."

"You have a point. But I sure hope it is the former rather than the latter."

"Definitely. At least this time we are in a cave, and there aren't dinosaurs looking to make a meal of us."

Red laughed. "Do you remember the last time when that dinosaur sneezed on you? The look on your face was priceless."

"Har har, you try getting dinosaur snot off of your jacket, it is not easy!"

"Oh I have," Red said with a wink.

"Oh you are going to get it."

"Promises promises."

"That is a guarantee my darling." James said as he added another log to the fire.

They both heard a soft beep. "Sounds like Atrus is done charging."

"Yes perhaps we both can get some rest now."

Red rubbed James' thigh. "Oh ... well there are other things we could do." She grinned.

"Love don't you need to rest?"

"I need you more though."

James leaned forward and kissed her deeply. "And I always need you."

After awhile James sat up and Red pulled him back down. "Hey, I am not done with you Mr. Moknkin."

He smiled and kissed her deeply, passionately. "Love I think we had better get *some* rest, don't you think?"

Red sighed. "Yes you are right. Plenty of time for that later. And believe me you are going to get it."

"Promises promises." James said as he removed Atrus and pressed the bottom of the cylindrical. There was another soft beep, and he appeared.

"Thank you Sir, I have a full charge. If you wish to rest now, I can keep watch."

James pulled Red close under the thermal blanket. "Thanks Atrus," he yawned. "Let us know if anyone or anything comes in range."

"Acknowledged."

James awoke twice to add wood to the fire and check with Atrus. When the sun peeked over the horizon Red awoke fully refreshed. James, while feeling better, his body still complained wanting a real night sleep in an actual bed.

Red sat up and stretched. "Come on sleepy head."

James pulled the blanket over his head. "Morning already?"

"I know you are not a morning person so I will go get us some water." Red said as she pulled out two expanding bottles from their packs and stood up.

"Deal, just be careful okay?"

"My darling this is not my first jump you know."

"Sorry love. You know I didn't mean anything by it."

"I know, you worry. And I think it is sweet." She said bending down to kiss his forehead then headed out and down the country side. After a bit she found a small stream and quickly filled the bottles. They beeped showing that the water was now safe, and she started walking back when she heard an unearthly sound. A cross between a shriek and a moan. A beller that turned her blood to ice. "No it is not possible!"

James popped his head up. "Atrus did you hear something?"

Atrus appeared before him. "Yes but what I heard is impossible."

"The wasteland creatures?"

"Yes, they have a very unique sound. I have never encountered anything else like it."

"Nor have we." James said standing up and quickly dressing. "Where did it come from?"

"I do not detect anything in range."

At first Red felt rather than saw it. Across the way a creature, just like she remembered, a lizard head and a cat body with talons similar to a raptor and covered in mostly iridescent scales. She took several slow steps back, but it already saw her and she knew it. She turned and bolted. "James!"

James heard and was at the cave entrance when he saw Red running at tremendous speed across the grass heading for them. And right behind her, a creature running faster than he thought was possible. "No, it can't be!" Red put on another burst of speed and she was in the cave in half a second. James wasted no time he drew the gun, flipped off the safety and aimed. The creature was almost on them when he fired point-blank. A raw cone of energy burst from the gun and slammed into the creature. It tried to fight the immense power, but it had no chance. The power blasted clean through the creature blowing apart muscle, blood, and bone. A second later it evaporated as though it had never been.

"Oh James!" Red said as she wrapped her arms around him and squeezed hard.

"I know I know. How the heck was that thing here? It shouldn't even have existed. We stopped the nuclear war that created them. And regardless they should be in the far future. Not now. Atrus, did you get a time fix via the stars last night?"

"Yes, we are in the target time-zone."

"Then how the heck is that thing here?"

Atrus shook his head. "I do not know, it is most puzzling," he said as his image winked out.

"I think I may have an idea. Keleeigan is doing more damage than I thought. He isn't just stopping us from jumping properly, the very barriers of time are breaking down. All things that could have happened, are bleeding through in all points of time. If we don't fix it when he appears next time, there won't be another chance at anything. It won't be that we can't jump again, it will be that the earth doesn't exist."

"Or it won't be the earth we know that is for sure," James said, "great, no pressure, eh?"

"Atrus?"

Atrus appeared before them. "Yes?"

"Why didn't you detect that creature before?"

"I do not know. I suspect it was due to being slightly outside of my range."

"Then why didn't you detect the tiger in the cave? That was certainly in your range."

"Well Sir, if you recall, I did."

"Yes you told me something was in there. In the past you told me details. What is going on?"

"I do not know."

"I want answers. Are you malfunctioning?"

"I do not believe so."

"Can you run a self diagnostic?"

"I can, but they run automatically on a regular basis."

"Do one now."

"I will need to shut down while this intensive diagnostician runs."

"Do it!"

"Acknowledged," Atrus said as his image flickered out.

Red looked at him as they headed back to towards the cave. "Do you really think he is malfunctioning?"

"I don't know, but twice he should have seen something and didn't. And we need to know one way or the other."

An hour later Atrus beeped and James pushed the button on the bottom of the cylinder. Atrus appeared before them. "I believe I have an answer for you."

James crossed his arms and glared. "Which is?"

"The first incident with the tiger, I indeed did have a slight variation in my main sensor network. Automatic diagnostics found the fault and corrected the calibration error."

"And the second?"

"That was not my error."

James eyes narrowed further. "How? You didn't detect that creature."

"That is correct; however, it is not due to the creature approaching by normal means and I failed to detect him. Temporal analysis shows the creature was simply not there one minute, and running after Red the next. Apparently it crossed the barriers of time and appeared here, very similar to us traveling through a warp. I could not have detected the creature before it was originally seen."

"I see." James leaned up against the cave wall and folded his arms.

"Atrus what caused the first problem?" Red asked

"That I do not know. A variation in my sensor network caused a calibration error for a short period."

"When did it happen?"

"When we were traveling in the warp before landing here."

James removed Atrus' cylinder from the pocket in his holster, sat it down and walked outside the cave. Red ran after him.

"Hey what is going on?"

"I don't know if I believe him. Twice in a row we could have died because he didn't tell us something was there."

Red grabbed his shoulders and looked into his eyes. "And if we didn't have him at all?"

"Well the first time we might have been killed."

"And the second you knew what was going on and came with the gun ready to incinerate the creature."

James looked down avoiding her eyes. "Yes."

She brought up a finger and turned his head so that their eyes met. "And how many times has he saved us before that?"

"Several."

"And do you think he is going to turn on us now?"

"Well ... I ... I just ... don't know."

"Look he may not be human but everyone makes mistakes. And I would say he more than made up for it. He did explain what happened, we both know that last jump rattled us. Apparently Atrus was no exception. And if you remember, it was *you* that wanted to bring him along in the first place," Red said smiling.

James smiled back and moved his shoulders back and forth in a swinging motion. "Yes you have a point."

"Good, at least we agree."

"It is just ... well ... I can't imagine my life without you."

Red framed his face with her hands and looked deep into his eyes. "Well my darling that is very mutual because I can't imagine life without you either. So what do we say we put this behind us and get back in there and formulate a plan?"

James gave her a squeeze. "Okay love, okay."

A few moments later they were sitting around the remains of the fire. "Atrus? Do you have any idea when Doc will show up?"

Atrus appeared before them and shook his head. "I am sorry. As I said before, I cannot tell you until there is a rise in temporal energy. The lighthouse's field is very unstable and hard to determine exactly where or when it will materialize."

Red sighed. "So we sit and wait … for now."

— 11 —

The lighthouse groaned under the tremendous temporal and physical assault. "Professor!" Trisia shouted. "Is there anything you can do?"

Keleeigan held on to one of the tables he had the good sense to bolt to the floor. He cringed as other tables fell over, shattering their delicate equipment.

"No! The field is even more unstable than last time. The lightning didn't help, it made things worse!"

"How?!"

The energy didn't make it to the accumulator I have in the lamp area, instead it fed directly into the temporal field. And because it was already unstable–"

"It made it a whole lot worse!" Trisia shouted.

"Yes!"

"There must be something you can do?" Kim shouted. "We can't keep going on like this!"

"No! But I don't know what we can do."

"There must be something!"

Keleeigan punched a few keys trying to hold on to his lunch and the table at the same time. "Well one good thing, this jump didn't drain the power cell any further like it has on previous jumps."

"How does that help?"

"If I bypass the normal energy distribution system and hot-wire the power cell directly to the accumulator. We might be able to punch through for a few minutes."

"And after that?"

Keleeigan shook his head. "After that we won't have enough energy to spit with much less pull us out of the warp. If we fall back in after this, there will be no leaving it … ever."

"Do it! This old building isn't going to hold together much longer!" Trisia shouted.

"All right." Keleeigan said while pointing to something on his screen. "Kim, I want you to hit this when I say. I am going to go downstairs, but don't do *anything* before I tell you!"

"Got it professor. Good luck."

"Luck my boy has nothing to do with science." He said getting to his feet and grabbed on the railing nearby made his way to the power room as fast as he could without falling. When he finally reached it, the level was low enough that the red light on the side flashed critical. He pulled one of the dead mains from the distribution system, plugged it directly into the power core, and switched it to run on the backup system inside the core. He hoped there was enough left, but the light was already flickering faster indicating the power level was a great deal lower than when he arrived.

"Kim! Hit it!" Keleeigan shouted.

"It is running! It says 'Warning: insufficient power and do I want to continue.'"

"Dang! Does it offer an option?"

"Other than yes or no. I have no options."

"We are in trouble!"

"We are out of power?"

"Just about. We don't have enough to do what I planned."

"So we are stuck here?"

"Unless you have any better ideas?"   The lighthouse groaned as it shook even more violently than before. "And make it fast."

"Professor you once told me you had invented a power booster that sped up power production by feed it through some crystals?"

"Yes. It was too unstable. Most of the time it blew sky-high."

"Do you have one?"

"Yes. But I never brought it here. It was too dangerous."

"Professor, where was it in your lab?"

"It was near the power cell before we brought it over. On the table right next to it in fact."

Trisia smiled. "Professor, remember when you asked me to pack up the power cell and bring it here?"

"Of course, what does this have to do–"

"I packed everything on that table too."

Keleeigan's eyes flashed. "*Everything*?"

"Yes everything."

"Where?"

"Should be down there, big brown box in the corner." Keleeigan looked around the room. There in the corner on the other side of the power cell was a big box. Keleeigan ripped it open to find his original booster, but he held back.

"It is too dangerous to use this, it will likely explode."

"So we either die now or later? I vote later!" Trisia shouted.

"I vote later too," Kim shouted down.

"All right! I will try!" Keleeigan said as he pulled out the strange squarish device containing several large multicolored crystals mounted in the exact center and attached it to the secondary lines of the power cell. A second later power flowed through the lines lighting them up. The booster's center glowed brighter and brighter as he ran back up the steps.

"It is in and building." Keleeigan said grabbing the railing and working his way back upstairs as fast as the lighthouse's jerking motion would allow.

"Great! Shall I hit this?" Kim said pointing.

"NO! Get your fingers away from that. I need to make adjustments and take the booster into consideration or it will blow for sure." Keleeigan said breathing hard as he sat down at the keyboard and began to issue commands faster than Kim could follow. The lighthouse shook again as a powerful wave of energy impacted its temporal field. They heard the cracks of tortured glass but it didn't quite shatter. Even though it was bulletproof and reinforced, there was no way it could withstand another impact like that.

"There! Hold on!" Keleeigan shouted as he engaged the booster system. Power built exceptionally inside the cell flashing it up to 75% but the cell was near the breaking point. "It is almost in thermal runaway. Jumping NOW!" He said jamming on a large button on his console. They felt a tremendous jolt as the lighthouse was shoved out of the warp and into normal space again. Keleeigan's fingers flew over the keys as he tried to shut down the booster. "Dang it! While the cell didn't run away due to the high power drain, the booster is still functioning and is starting another exponential build!" He ran for the stairs.

"What are you going to do?" Kim shouted after him.

"What I can!" Keleeigan ran down the steps out of breath and found the booster glowing brightly. Way too bright. He ran over and pulled one of the cables but it refused to budge. The massive amount of energy released in one microsecond had fused it to the cell. He looked at the indicators and any second it was going to explode.

The floor pitched under his feet and Keleeigan spun around. He spied an old fire axe with a long wooden handle still hanging on the wall. He grabbed it and swung with all of his might. The axe was rusty but sharp enough to cut through the cables with all of his force behind it. Sparks flew from the severed raw energy lines, then died. The booster itself began to dim, but it took several minutes before it reached safe levels again. Keleeigan threw the axe in the corner and sighed. "All this technology and I had to use an axe." He shook his head, turned, and started back up the stairs.

"What was that?" Kim called down.

"Me, having a meaningful talk with the booster."

"Talk? Sounded like you beat the heck out of it."

Keleeigan smiled. "Sort of," he said as he reached the top steps. "What's our status?"

"If this is right, we don't have enough power to jump again and the temporal field is still enclosing us."

Keleeigan sighed as he sat back down. "And now we wait."

"For?"

"A miracle."

— 12 —

After several hours Atrus appeared in front of them. "Yes Atrus?" James asked, "what is it?"

"I detect elevated levels of temporal displacement."

"Doc?"

"Considering I have not encountered anything else similar …yes."

Red stood up. "Where?"

"South of this position, forty meters before the stream."

"Not good, that is near where I saw that creature."

"Well you always told me they never give up once they have your scent. But I blasted that one to bits. It won't be bothering us."

"Yes. However, they never travel alone. We found that out remember?"

James sighed. "I remember, all too well. You thought they were solitary creatures, until then."

"And we found out how wrong I was. But in my defense I didn't stay around and watch them. I warped out of there as quick as I could. And I barely made it."

"Temporal disturbance increasing."

"Yes Atrus, we need to get down there." James said replacing the few items they had taken out of his backpack before removing Red's from the larger linen bag and handing it to her. "Figured you might want that." He grinned.

Red took it smiling. "Thanks, let's go." She said slinging it on her back.

They walked for a short time until they reached the stream. "Atrus? Anything in the area?"

Atrus flashed in front of them. "No, I do not detect anything in the vicinity."

"Good perhaps we have caught a break."

"I wouldn't be so sure, we both know how unpredictable those things are."

"True. Atrus? Where is that field you spoke of?"

"All around us. I suggest we move back fifty meters."

"Ohhh yes." James and Red said in unison as they ran back a bit.

"Sir, if I may make a suggestion, activate the Shell."

"Why?"

"Well if creatures approach I am more helpful with the Shell online. Or if we need its holographic abilities."

James nodded. "True, okay." He said pulling the Shell out of his pack, opening the panel, activating it, then sealing the panel. "Okay there you go."

"Acknowledged, I have control." Atrus said as the Shell hovered up off of James' hand and up to roughly head height.

"The temporal instability is growing rapidly. Brace yourselves."

"Keleeigan!" Trisia shouted as she fell backward, pulled herself up, and fought to stay on her feet. "This is insane! Can you do anything?"

"No! When I shoved us out last time we landed with enough force to rubber-band back into the warp, which I didn't think was possible. Just hang on. It should be all over in a minute, one way or the other." He said as the lighthouse shook and jerked this way and that.

"Professor when you say 'come on over for a wild time' you sure don't kid around," Kim said.

Keleeigan looked towards him. "I never said that!"

Kim smiled. "Well you should have!"

"Professor! I think I see something outside of the door, a break in this strange storm."

"Good! I hope we head towards it!"

"You mean you aren't driving?"

"No, only slightly influencing our path to where we were before. Nudging you could say. That is all I can do without that timing chip!"

"Well I think you are nudging right, we seem to be heading for it."

"Good! That point is the only place we can exit again. We don't have the power to create another. Brace yourselves, this is going to be rough."

The lighthouse slammed into the break bounced back then headed towards it again. This time though it pushed its way through. First just a little, then a little more, shaking and vibrating every which way as it did. With a giant bang it arrived on the plain. Red and James were thrown back with the displaced air.

James shook his head to clear it. "It is Doc!"

"Affirmative. The temporal field is still highly unstable. It is very probable it will start to pull him back in a few minutes," Atrus said.

James grabbed Red's hand, and they ran for the entrance on

the other side of the lighthouse. They found it with the door open and saw the same black-haired girl from before. "Get Doc!" James shouted. But she just looked at him cocking her head.

"Professor looks like we made it, I see grassy plain of some kind, a few scattered trees, a little stream and a forest beyond it."

"For now, until the warp pulls us back in." Keleeigan said checking their status his screen.

"Professor I see some guy here. Same guy as before, and he has a woman and some other guy with him. The other guy just flickered and reformed! What in the–"

"James?! We may have a chance!" Keleeigan said as he bolted for the door causing his chair to spin around and fall over with the sudden movement.

The temporal field was still covering the lighthouse, the aura increased as the instability grew. "James! You need to stabilize the field and get in here!" He shouted several times but James only looked at him.

"Doc! How can we help you?" James shouted but to no avail, then looked towards Red. "He still can't hear me."

"As I have mentioned before, the temporal field blocks many wavelengths including those of sound," Atrus said.

"I wish we could understand him," Red said.

Atrus looked more carefully at Keleeigan as he began to do motions and kept talking. "I believe I understand what he is trying to tell us."

"Well don't hold us in suspense!"

"He wants Red to run around the lighthouse in a clockwise

direction and try generating a warp. He hopes this will stabilize the field allowing you to get inside and give him the components he requires."

James turned towards Red. "Do you think it will work?"

Red shrugged. "I have no idea. But worth a try. The alternative is all of time and space breaks down."

"Okay, I will get right next to the field. You run around and try to get it stable. Hopefully I can get in after." James said then pointed to the Shell. "Atrus better bring that down here."

"Actually Sir, I have another suggestion. It can go up higher and shouldn't be affected by Red attempting to create a warp."

"But why? There is no point."

"But there is. I detect more creatures on the very edge of my scanners. They do not seem to be heading directly here, but I suspect it is only a matter of time. With the Shell deployed I can hold them off if need be."

Red sighed. "He has a point."

"All right, just keep it up high."

"I will Sir."

Red lowered herself into a sprinting position.

"Ready?"

"*Go!*" James shouted.

Red bolted running at high speed and the air began to swirl.

Inside Trisia squinted as she saw Red running faster and faster around the lighthouse. "What in the world is she doing?"

"Yess! They got my message! She is going to stabilize the field. If it is enough James should be able to get in here."

"How is that going to help?"

"My dear, he has a new chip and a power supply we can use to go home!"

Trisia's eyes flashed. "What? How in the world did he know to bring them? Or better yet how did he follow us?"

"Never mind." Keleeigan said going back to his console and tapped several buttons. "She is doing it! The field is stabilizing!"

Outside the wind whipped as Red increased her speed again.

"Sir, the temporal field is stabilizing."

"Red!" James shouted, "keep it up!"

"Trying!" she shouted as she ran past.

"Sir the creatures are approaching."

"How many?"

"Three." Atrus said but James could see them in the distance approaching fast. "They will be here in ten seconds."

Inside Trisia pointed out the door in fear and shock. "What in the world are those things!"

Keleeigan ran over to see what she was pointing at. "Oh my, I have never seen anything like them. They look like mutants, but this isn't a post nuclear war torn area. And they are heading right for James."

"Atrus, can you take them out with the Shell?" James asked.

"I will endeavor to do so." Atrus said as the Shell lowered and aimed. The creatures were running fast but Atrus took the first one out with ease. Another shrieked as it continued running fast. The Shell's powerful beam weapon glowed with power before it unleashed its deadly energy bolt. It slammed into the second one vaporizing it.

"Don't waste the power vaporizing them. Use low power shots. Stun if you have to."

"Acknowledged." Atrus said as another beam, this time far less in diameter slammed into the third and final one dropping it like a big sack of meat. "Situation handled and Sir, the field will be stable enough for you to try to enter in ten seconds."

James turned around and saw that most of the shimmer from the temporal field had dissipated leaving only a slight hue emanating from the lighthouse.

"Red you okay?" James said as he saw the fatigue already on Red's face as she ran past.

"Go! Hurry!"

James jumped through the doorway and landed on the wooden floor with a thud. Trisia and Kim stood there with their mouths agape.

"James! The chip! Hurry!" Keleeigan said quickly.

James whipped his bag off of his back, reached in, found the chip in its protective case and tossed it over to Keleeigan who caught it in midair.

"Thank you!" He said opening the chip's protective case, sliding out the board with the bad chip, popping it off of the board, slipping the new chip in, and sliding the board back into place. "There! Now toss me the gun!"

"The gun?? But–"

"Don't argue! Do it now!" Keleeigan said.

James sighed and tossed the weapon over to Keleeigan who opened the control panel, input a code, the screen beeped then slid out revealing the power cell behind it. Keleeigan held it up. "Perfect! I will be right back." He said running down the stairs. Fifteen seconds later he appeared again. "Okay it is all hooked up. Now we hope it's enough," Keleeigan said as he punched several keys on his console.

"Sir?"

"Yes Atrus?"

Atrus appeared in front of James. "I detect more creatures approaching fast."

"How many?"

"Too many for me to take them all out with the Shell's current power reserve."

"Great," James snorted, "just when I thought things were going so well."

"Who the heck is that?" Trisia asked pointing.

Atrus turned towards Trisia. "I am Artificial Technological Renovational Universal Sys–"

"Never mind, take too long to explain, just know he is with me and a friend," James said.

"Dang it!" Keleeigan said as he banged his fist on the table. "We still don't have enough power. Almost but not quite. We were so close."

"Guys…whatever…you…are…going…to…do…you …had …better …do …it …soon. I …can't …keep …this …up …much …longer!" Red shouted each word as she passed the doorway.

Atrus raised his hand. "Sir if I may offer a suggestion."

"What is it?" James said turning to face him.

"Professor Keleeigan, do you still have any of those weather balloons you used before?"

Keleeigan nodded. "Yes one left, why? We need a lightning storm for them to be of any use."

Atrus smiled. "But Miss Red can make that storm for you."

Keleeigan grinned. "That might be enough, if one of her bolts hits the balloon, and it flowed into the accumulator–"

"We could warp out of here?" James asked.

Keleeigan nodded. "It is a long shot but the only one we have."

"Guyyyyys!" Red shouted

James went to the door. "Red! Can you create a warp?"

"I ... don't ... know ... tired!"

"Try! We need a lightning bolt to push this thing home."

"Will ... see ... what ... I ... can ... do."

"Sir the creatures are nearly here."

"Hold them off as best you can Atrus."

"Acknowledged." Atrus said as a beam lashed out and hit one of the creatures head-on. It fell, the others stopped but only for a moment then started running again even faster than before.

"Take out another."

"Target acquired." Atrus said as a beam hit another creature but this time the beam passed through the first and hit the second taking both down in a heap.

"What did you do?"

"I got 'creative' Sir, using the same energy bolt. I figured that if I increased the power slightly it would pass through one creature and into the one behind it. In this fashion it took less power than two low power shots."

"Good thinking."

More beams shot out taking down several other creatures which streaked in response and stopped their approach.

"Good that seems to slowed them down for a few minutes."

"And how does that do us any good? They will be here in a moment and we are still not heading home," Trisia said.

"Red we could use that lightning about now!" James said leaning out the doorway.

"Shut ... it! Am ... trying!" She shouted back and pushed a little harder.

Keleeigan hit another button on his console and his final

balloon launched up into the sky. "Balloon is away, it is up to her now."

Dark clouds swirled around the lighthouse as Red continued to run. She pushed little harder, and the air sparked. She pushed again, and it sparked again.

"Not … sure … if … I … can … so … very … tired."

"You can do it love! Just once more."

"Okay … will … try."

She pushed once more and a large bolt shot down and struck the balloon. The power vaporized the balloon instantly and traveled down the wire into the power accumulator. It started to glow brighter and brighter.

"She did it!" Keleeigan said as the building shook.

"Sir the creatures are approaching again."

"Atrus do what you can."

"Acknowledged." Atrus said as the Shell shot out again and again. It took down several creatures, but more were on the horizon and approaching fast.

"Red! Get in here!" James shouted

"Okay." She shouted back and ran for the door but nearly fainted.

"Sir more creatures are approaching."

"I see them." James said looking numerous shapes approaching at high speed. "Do what you can."

More beams lanced out taking out several, but still more creatures remained. "I cannot remove any more unless I use the emergency reserve of the Shell."

James sighed. "Do it! We can't let them get in here. Doc how long?"

"The jump sequence is building … less than a minute."

Two more red beams shot out from the Shell killing four

more creatures but three more still remained. The Shell, its power exhausted, fell from the sky.

The lighthouse shook again. "Power at max! Red! Get in here! Hold on to something everyone, we are jumping!" Keleeigan shouted over the electronic sparking and the groan of the building itself as it began to shake. He punched the large button on his console causing energy to surge from the smaller power cell, into the main, and from there into the accumulator. Red used the very last of her energy and managed to run through the doorway, colliding with James as they both went down in a tumble. The building shook and groaned as it lurched from normal space just as two creatures jumped for the door.

Everyone tried to hold on as the lighthouse shook and jerked this way and that. James held on to Red who had already fell asleep in his arms, beyond exhausted.

"Is she okay?" Trisia asked looking at Red.

"Yes, at least I think so. Opening warps really drains her. She should be fine once she rests a bit."

Trisia snorted. "That is if we make it."

"Doc? How are we doing?"

Keleeigan kept staring at his screen never turning. "We are heading back to our own time. At least I think so."

"You *THINK* so?" Trisia shouted.

"Well my dear, a lot of this equipment has been overloaded, patched, strained to the breaking point, and patched again. With the chip in place we should be traveling towards the future, but a lot of my sensors were fried in that last jump we did so I can't be certain."

"Atrus?"

Atrus flashed on in front of James. "Yes Sir?"

"Can you tell if we are on course?"

"Yes we are heading forward, that much I am certain. I can't give you an exact time fix though as we are moving."

"Give me a rough guess," Keleeigan said.

"I deal with precision, I do not–"

"Atrus?" James grunted.

"Yes?"

"Answer him," James said as his eyes narrowed.

"Very well, 600 AD and increasing."

"Good thank you. I may not be able to get us back at the precise moment we left, but it should be close. While I can't tell our exact position, the homing feature I built in last minute seems to be holding."

Kim raised an eyebrow. "Homing feature?"

"Yes I figured if someone was doing time travel, and jumped around several time-lines, they would want to go back to where they were originally, when they started their trip and not accidentally encounter themselves. I assume that would be very bad."

James chuckled. "You got that right."

Keleeigan spun around in his chair. "What!? Did you actually do it?"

"No, but Red has. Or as close as you ever want to get, trust me on that."

Keleeigan nodded running his fingers through his white hair. "I do my boy, I do. And I have no doubt encountering yourself is never a good idea when time traveling. Why the consequences are almost limitless, and none of them good."

James nodded. "Red still doesn't know, and she has been doing this far longer than anyone."

The lighthouse shook again and tortured super structure groaned. One of the overhead beams showed a growing crack. Kim wiped the sweat from his forehead. "Professor, how much longer? You said we couldn't take much more of those, and that was quite a while ago."

Keleeigan laughed. "Not much longer my boy, and this building is like me, a tough old bird. She will hold together."

"You hope," Trisia said.

"We all hope, or at least I would assume everyone feels the same my dear."

"Oh I do, I can't wait for this ride to end." Trisia said while still holding on to the nearby railing with one hand and her stomach with the other.

The lighthouse shuddered again but this time it felt different. "Professor Keleeigan, I detect a decrease in speed inside the warp. Our progression through time has slowed by a large margin," Atrus said.

Keleeigan turned back to his console and hit several keys. "Dang it! We are losing power faster than we should."

"Why?"

"Wish I knew! Could be this equipment or the power cell is giving up the ghost, I don't know. I certainly didn't intend on torturing my equipment like this. I just wanted one small test jump."

"Next time take spare parts!" James laughed.

"Oh my boy I plan on keeping spare parts for the spare parts! Dang it, power is dropping even faster now."

"Will it last?"

"Hope so!"

"Based on various projections we have a 48% chance the energy will be depleted before we reach our intended target," Atrus said.

"Atrus?" James said.

"Yes Sir?"

"Shut it!"

"But Sir, I thought that everyone would want to know."

"Doc yes, the rest of us, no. And I think Doc already knows."

"Yes he is right, although I gave us 56% so I like his odds better."

James rolled his eyes and sighed. "Great."

"We are almost there, I think." Keleeigan said his fingers dancing over the keys.

"Should we stop early and recharge?"

"My boy, after all I have put this power cell through, I am not going to trust it being able to fire another jump. If we stop now, we may never get home.

"Almost there … a few more seconds … hang on we are jumping out!" Keleeigan said as he pushed another button that shoved every ounce of energy into the accumulator. The power compressed and slammed directly into the temporal field strengthening it.

A tear appeared nearby and grew in size. First doubling, then tripling until finally it was large enough to swallow the lighthouse. It came like a hungry mouth engulfing the building. Everyone felt their stomachs lurch even stronger than before as they were pulled between time-zones and were spit out landing with a mighty crash. Sparks flew between various consoles causing several to explode. With the energy exhausted, the temporal field collapsed ending their wild ride.

Kim ran over to the door and looked out. He smiled when he saw his car, just as he left it. "Bull's eye Professor!"

Keleeigan stood and stretched. "Whew, next time I am going to leave the testing to someone else."

James smiled. "But if you did, no one would have got back."

Keleeigan nodded. "True but still. This kind of thing is for the younger."

James grinned. "Hey weren't you the one that just said you were a tough old bird?"

"I am, but emphasis on *old*."

"Nah, Doc you are only as old as you feel."

Keleeigan stretched again and heard several pops from complaining muscles and bones. "In that case I feel about five hundred."

"Well, actually, if you are basing that on years traveled you are well over several million."

"Atrus?" James said.

"Yes Sir?"

"Drop it."

Atrus nodded. "Yes Sir."

Red stirred in James' arms as her eyes fluttered open. He looked into those dark blue pools and smiled. "Are you okay love?"

"Mmmm yes, tired with one big headache."

"I am not surprised actually, you opened a warp in a very unusual manner. Well unusual for you that is," Keleeigan said.

Atrus raised his hand. "Professor, if I may ask, what caused your problem in the first place? While I know it was a failure of the timing chip, I am surprised such a failure would occur."

"So am I Atrus. I can't imagine what could have burned it out like it did. There shouldn't have been enough power to do that. The chip itself is very failure redundant and the board it is mounted in is has nowhere near that kind of energy."

Atrus walked over and looked at the timing board that was now carefully mounted inside its normal housing, then at the burnt chip on the table nearby. James opened his jacket further as he itched a spot on his upper right shoulder, revealing Atrus' cylinder still in the holster pocket. A green beam shot from it covering the housing and chip then retracting.

"Atrus? Next time just ask," James said frowning.

"Sorry Sir I thought I would take advantage of the opportunity. Hmm yes I agree, the current power supply is not enough to generate the kind of damage I see on this chip."

"Exactly. I assumed that I must have missed something in the power regulation that when the system was fully powered, it crashed through and fried the chip."

"Still it should not have created quite this much damage." Atrus said as his scanning beam lanced out again and went over the chip several more times. "That is very strange."

Keleeigan walked over. "What is?"

"While this chip was indeed damaged by power overload, but by a direct power strike and for a sustained amount of time. My estimation is for five minutes or more."

Keleeigan raised an eyebrow. "Impossible! A small power arc for a second, perhaps. But there were never any shorts for over five minutes!"

"Indeed. Nor do I see any signs that such a power surge happened inside the casing. If such a surge did happen, it would have damaged many more components, not this single chip."

"It would have fried the entire board, and perhaps everything in the case."

Atrus nodded. "Exactly. This appears to have been done deliberately."

Keleeigan's eyes went wide. "Deliberately? That is not possible!"

"Why not?"

"Because no one even knew of this project, except for Kim and Trisia. And they both went with me."

"Hmm that is most puzzling," Atrus said still facing the chip. "However, I see Trisia inching towards the door. I suspect she has more information on this matter."

Everyone whirled around to see Trisia almost to the door. "Trisia? You did this?"

The young woman looked around, looked towards the door, looked back at them, and seemed to come to a decision. "You bet I did!"

"Why? You would be trapped just as much as I."

"If you remember I wasn't planning on being here, and you activated the jump sequence without asking me! You just did it! I wasn't supposed to be here, I was going out on a date remember?"

"Why didn't you say something?"

"And say what? Hmm? 'Oh Professor don't jump now as I sabotaged your main system and you will never be able to return'?"

"But why would you do this? You have been working on this project just as hard as I."

"Because my name isn't Trisia Swain, it's Sanford!"

Keleeigan's eyes went wide. "Linus' daughter!"

"Yes the daughter you orphaned when you took him from me! He was all that I had left in the world!"

"But I didn't kill him. I tried to warn him."

"Ha! That is what they all say. He left me information, drives full of data on what you really did. Reading through it my anger only grew. I spent the past ten months trying to get close enough to you and waited for the right moment. When you started on this time travel kick, I knew it was the perfect time."

"But I checked your background."

"What can I say, genius runs in the family." Trisia said with a flick of her hand. "I made a persona that I knew you would like to help you in your research. Then modified all the records to match. A simple procedure really."

"I am sure," Atrus said.

"Atrus?" James said out the corner of his mouth.

"Yes Sir?"

"Not now!"

"Yes Sir."

"But my dear, I didn't hurt him. Whatever data he gave you is flawed. I did my best to try to warn him that the cloaking system was deadly."

"Hardly! What you told him only encouraged him more!"

"I told him the truth, I can't help it if he didn't listen."

James sat Red's drowsy form carefully to the side. "Listen Doc would never hurt anyone. I even saw Sanford, he was beyond reason. He was trying to kill the president after all."

"Only because the president was destroying this country and no one was going to act!"

James shook his head. "No you have that wrong. I have been to the future when Sanford was successful. It was anything but better. Sanford initiated a line of events that caused the world to go into full nuclear war. The world was nothing but a wasteland after that."

"I don't believe you!"

"Believe what you want, but I was there. I saw the destruction. The mutants running around, cities reduced to rubble. The human race destroyed."

Trisia jabbed a finger in James' face. "You still killed him just as much as Keleeigan."

James shook his head. "I had nothing to do with his death. In fact I didn't even fire a shot."

"You didn't? But I heard–What did happen then?"

James sighed. "Red and I stopped him from killing the president, then he ran into the residential section of the White House. I found him in one of the unoccupied rooms and tried to talk him down. But there was no reasoning with him. I finally got him to turn off the cloak, but he was too far gone."

Trisia blinked. "Too far gone?"

James nodded. "Yes I could see right through him even with the cloak off. He finally realized it when he could see through his hand to the floor below. He freaked, as anyone would, and asked for me to get Doc. But there wasn't time. And even if there was, it was too late. He was coming apart, dissolving away into nothingness. There wasn't any way to reverse the process."

Trisia's eyes grew cold. "Did you try?"

"What?"

"Did you even try to save him?"

"I already told you it was too late to do anything."

"But did you even try?"

"And do what? I didn't have any equipment on me. And even if I did, according to Doc his DNA along with everything else was unraveling. There was nothing that could be done."

"But you didn't try!"

"Try how?"

"I don't know, you could have tried. You could have done something!"

"Trisia, it was like watching someone going over a waterfall. I could do nothing but watch. Sure I wanted to, but there was nothing that I could do."

Trisia sighed. "Perhaps–No! You did it intentionally and I am going to prove it." She said backing towards the door.

"My dear, James is telling the truth. There was nothing that I or anyone could do. I wish I could have helped him. And I did try. Linus was one of my closest friends for years. It was his obsession over the cloaking system that split us up. But I never stopped caring, and I did try to keep track of him and how he was doing. No major spying you understand, just enough to see that he was okay and roughly where he was.

"I admit now that if I had been watching more carefully, then perhaps I would have known what he was up to long ago. But I doubt I could have changed his mind. I tried many times in the past and he always thought I was skewing the data so I could have the technology for myself.

"Heck if I did, don't you think that the technology would have been in my lab? Or I would have a patent on it?"

"That is because you wanted to keep it quiet." Trisia said taking another step backward towards the door.

"Of course I did! I didn't want anyone else trying to duplicate Linus' work and die in the process because they thought it could be done. I do think that cloaking technology will work eventually, but with a different method. The one he used is deadly.

"If I wanted it, I could have had helped him with it. Way back in the day we shared everything. I didn't want it and I hoped that us going our separate ways would have shown him how serious I was, and how deadly the device would be. But it seems it only strengthened his resolve to prove me wrong."

"So you admit it! You killed him!"

"I didn't kill him my dear. I could have handled things differently, but in the end, I don't think it would make any difference. He was too stubborn to listen."

"I don't believe you!" Trisia said bolting for the door covering the rest of the distance in a heartbeat. James ran and tackled her but she kicked him on the side of the head making him see stars. He shook his head and silently cursed forgetting one of the carnal rules of the FBI to never trust a girl in a short skirt, she will use it to her advantage and more often than not, surprise you.

"She …is …getting away." James said still shaking his head trying to clear it.

"Allow me Sir," Atrus said. As they watched a red beam shot down from above and knocking the girl unconscious. She fell forward getting a face full of dirt.

James stumbled forward a bit as he tried to get up. "The Shell?"

Atrus nodded. "Correct Sir."

"But I thought you lost it in the last jump?"

"No, I said that its power was exhausted and it would fall. It did, but I positioned it so that it would fall between the railing and the glass structure that encircles the light area at the top of this building."

"But the power supply was exhausted?"

"It was, but it self-recharged just enough for one small stun shot. Which you saw."

"Well I for one am heading home," Kim said heading towards the door. "I have had enough adventure for quite a while. Not to mention find out that Trisia almost stopped me from seeing anymore ever again."

"Far more than that. It almost stopped everyone from ever seeing anything ever again," James said.

Keleeigan cocked an eyebrow. "What do you mean?"

"Do you remember the odd creatures?"

"Yes, what were they?"

"Well the temporal field was so unstable that the barriers of time were actually breaking down. Things that shouldn't exist were slipping through the cracks. Those creatures shouldn't have existed as Red and I stopped the war that created them. And yet there they were."

"I can't image my field doing that. Granted it was unstable, but it had that much of a toxic effect on the continuum?"

James nodded. "Yes. We never would have thought it was possible either. It might have been an odd quirk of your field. Or it could have been the instability."

Atrus raised his hand. "I think that is far more likely than the field itself having a barrier breaking effect."

Keleeigan nodded. "I agree. I can't imagine the field itself causing harm. Or even anything beyond passing through the warp itself."

"Unless it was due to the size," James said.

"I suspect it was a combination of elements, size, instability, and power fluctuations," Atrus said.

Red reached over and pulled at James' pant leg. "Help me up?"

"Are you sure you are okay?"

"I am fine, just very tired. But better than I was. Now help me up."

James laughed. "Of course love, of course," he said helping her to her feet.

"Why don't you two rest at my home? I have a new one not far from here, I even had a swimming pool put in."

"Are you sure Doc? We don't want to intrude."

"Intrude? You just pulled my bacon out of the fire! It is the least I can do. Let me drive you over." Keleeigan pulled out his keys.

James smiled as he turned towards the doorway. "Okay, you talked us into it. Wait, where is Trisia?" James said pointing.

Outside she was nowhere to be seen. Only a slight mark in the dirt remained.

"Dang it, she got away!" James said looking around. "Atrus I thought you stunned her?"

"I did Sir; however, the power reserves in the Shell had still not built up to normal levels. Apparently, I underestimated the effectiveness of that last shot."

Keleeigan smiled. "Don't worry about her my boy. She can't do anything."

"She could steal the equipment that is here if we leave."

"Ha! Most of it is junk now. And anyway all the real data about it is back in my lab. She couldn't get it working, let alone fix it without that."

"But what about the computers here?"

"They are all in lock down with triple encryption. If they still work at all. That last surge fired most of everything here."

"The power cell?"

"Toast, well the main one. Which reminds me." Keleeigan said heading down the steps. He returned a minute later holding the small gun power cell, reinstalled it into the weapon, and offered it to James. "Here, you might want this."

James took it and smiled then placed it back in his holster

while continuing to balance Red as she leaned against him. "Thanks Doc."

"You are welcome my boy, now I think Red could use a long soak in my hot tub," Keleeigan said grinning.

Red's head bobbed up. "Hot tub?"

Keleeigan laughed. "Yes I think she will live." As they left, he turned around, pulled out a different key with a button and inserted it into the lock. A faint click was heard in addition to several electronic sounds.

"Doc? What was all of that?"

"Well you were afraid of what Trisia might do with my equipment. I don't think anything of value is in there now. But I don't see any reason to take chances either. I locked the door and activated the security system."

"Security system?"

"Just a little something I rigged up, and it seems to still work." Keleeigan said placing the key remote back in his pocket.

James shuddered. "If it is anything like your system at the lab, this thing will now be more secure than Fort Knox."

Keleeigan laughed. "Not that well my boy, but it should keep her, and anyone else out until I get back."

James opened the green door on Keleeigan's hybrid electric and carefully placed Red in the back seat. She immediately lay down and went to sleep. Keleeigan slipped into the driver's seat and started the engine. "Still like these hybrid electrics eh Doc?"

"Of course, and they present an almost endless opportunity for modification."

James' eyes went wide. "Don't tell me you modified the overdrive in this one too?"

Keleeigan laughed.   "No, of course not, that wasn't practical. However, hover mode is."

"Hover mode? What–" James asked but never had a chance to finish as the wheels rotated so that the rims faced the ground and jets activated propelling the car upwards.

As the car climbed into the sky, a shadowy figure emerged from behind a tree. The shadow opened a hand revealing a small data drive. She smiled and quickly closed her hand around it, then slipped the drive into her pocket. It was only a tiny spark, but a spark is all one needs.

About The Author

Don is the author of six science fiction novels and many more short stories. He lives in the USA where he continues to dream up more fantastic worlds for you to enjoy. When not writing, he can usually be found devouring another science fiction book, TV series, or movie.

Other works by Don DeBon:

Italian Fever

A real vacation. Crystal had looked forward to this for a long time. A little trip to Italy, relaxing on a cruise ship, being catered to and pampered. Something she has always dreamed of. But little did she know that it was going to turn out to be far more of an adventure than she had planned.

And now she is jet-setting all over the world with a man she just met for something that could change the world as we know it. Can she trust him? Her head says no but the heart says yes...

Red Warp

In a race against time the casualty could be your life.

If you could travel through time with just yourself and no machine needed, would you?

Meet Red, a woman with a amazing gift, the gift of passing though time and space without the need of any bulky equipment. The places she has seen, the people she has helped will blow your mind.

Now meet James, just your average newly minted FBI agent minding his own business until he is thrust headlong into Red's world. A world he didn't ask for, but one that hit him in the face full force. Can they get along long enough to survive?

Soulmates

Mechands . . . everyone has one. The metal race built by man to serve our every need. But Aleshia is about to find out they are not the benevolent protectors that she has always been taught. And who is this strange man in her dreams? The man who actually exists and reveals the whole world is not as she thought.

Word of mouth is crucial for authors. If you enjoyed this book, would you consider leaving a review? It is very much appreciated.

Amazon USA

http://www.amazon.com/

Amazon UK

http://www.amazon.co.uk/

Goodreads
http://www.goodreads.com/

Connect with the Author
Email: writer.don.debon@gmail.com
Mailing List: http://eepurl.com/bxWAov
Website: http://www.dondebon.com
Twitter: @DonDeBon
Google+: +DonDeBon

**This Edition Published 2015 by
DBDigital Publishing**

**ISBN 978-0-9881783-7-3
ISBN 978-0-9881783-5-9 (e-book)**

www.ingramcontent.com/pod-product-compliance
Lightning Source LLC
Chambersburg PA
CBHW070011120726
47909CB00003B/885